Diane Warner's

COMPLETE BOOK

OF

BABY

Showers

**Hundreds of Ways to Host
a Unique Celebration**

By
Diane Warner

CAREER PRESS
3 Tice Road
P.O. Box 687
Franklin Lakes, NJ 07417
1-800-CAREER-1
201-848-0310 (NJ and outside U.S.)
Fax: 201-848-1727

DIANE WARNER'S COMPLETE BOOK OF BABY SHOWERS
Cover design by Tom Phon
Printed in the U.S.A. by Book-mart Press

To order this title, please call toll-free 1-800-CAREER-1 (NJ and Canada: 201-848-0310) to order using VISA or Master-Card, or for further information on books from Career Press.

Library of Congress Cataloging-in-Publication Data

Warner, Diane.
    [Complete book of baby showers]
    Diane Warner's complete book of baby showers : hundreds of ways to host a unique celebration / by Diane Warner.
        p.   cm.
    Includes index.
    ISBN 1-56414-336-8 (pbk.)
    1. Showers (Parties)--Planning.   2. Infants.   I. Title.
GV1472.7.S5W37   1998
793.2--dc21   98-10647

Also by Diane Warner

The Best Wedding Ever

Complete Book of Wedding Vows

Complete Book of Wedding Toasts

Complete Book of Wedding Showers

How to Have a Big Wedding on a Small Budget

*Big Wedding on a Small Budget
Planner and Organizer*

*Beautiful Wedding Decorations and Gifts
on a Small Budget*

*How to Have a Fabulous, Romantic
Honeymoon on a Budget*

*Picture-Perfect Worry-Free Weddings:
71 Destinations & Venues*

Acknowledgments

Many thanks to all of you who agreed to share your party ideas with my readers, with special thanks to Janice Burroughs, Michele Perry, Karen Hilgers, Shari Green, Lisa Warner, Lynn Paden, Linda Glass, Carrie Hilgers, Beth Bryan, and Denise Rolls.

I am also grateful to my editors at Career Press—Betsy Sheldon, Ellen Scher, and Gloria Fuzia—for their help in putting this book together.

Contents

Introduction

I don't know which is more fun to host, a bridal shower or a baby shower. A bridal shower is exciting, of course, because we love to bask in the glow radiating from the bride-to-be. A baby shower, on the other hand, is a time to celebrate the fruit of a couple's love: a baby. And not just any baby, but a *special* baby, because it's *their* baby. I'm absolutely convinced that every expectant parent honestly believes that no one has ever experienced such an awesome blessing, such a special event, which is why a baby shower is such a happy occasion, a chance to share the couple's joy and shower them with gifts for their precious baby.

A baby shower is also an opportunity to pamper the guests of honor. Once the baby arrives, it may be quite a while before the new parents have the time, money, and energy to indulge in the luxury of a night out, so why not treat them to something special?

Whatever happened to the traditional ladies' klatch where the guests enjoy a simple dessert and coffee as they watch the mother-to-be open her gifts? Well, they still exist, especially in the South and Midwest, but a few new trends have developed as well, especially along the West Coast and in the larger metropolitan areas of the country. For one thing, there are more co-ed parties than there used to be, due partly to the fact that daddies have become more involved in the childbirth process. Not only are they attending natural childbirth classes and assisting in the delivery rooms, but they are also more interested in their babies' care. So, doesn't it make sense to include them in the baby showers? And, because a co-ed shower honors both expectant parents, it tends to be more of a "party" and less of a traditional baby shower.

Parties given exclusively for the daddy-to-be, which are often planned by his close buddies as a "last night out with the boys" before the baby arrives, or hosted over the lunch hour by his co-workers, are another way to honor the father's new role.

Then, of course, there are still the traditional "Mommy" parties, where the mommy-to-be is showered with gifts for her new baby. The difference is that today's baby showers are more lively and creative than they used to be.

The nice thing about any modern baby shower is that there are no strict rules to follow, and the shower may be hosted by anyone— friend, relative, or co-worker. As a matter of fact, it is often co-hosted by two or three people, which is much less stressful and costly than doing everything single-handedly. However, not everyone is a natural hostess, able to throw a party together with very little effort, and some of us are so stressed out at work that we have very little time to plan a party.

Whatever your hostess profile, I have good news for you: You'll find this book filled with fresh new ideas guaranteed to make your baby shower a success. You'll find everything from party themes, to creative invitations and decorations, to popular new games and menus, as well as easy worksheets to keep you organized.

Have fun as you explore the ideas and plan a memorable baby shower!

Part I

Choosing the Theme

The first step in planning a baby shower is to choose the theme, because the theme will determine everything else, from the party's location, to the games and decorations, to the type of food and drink that will be served. In this section, I have included themes for family parties, women-only parties, men-only parties, co-ed parties, as well as several types of special parties, such as those honoring a first-time grandmother, the arrival of twins (or triplets!), or a couple expecting a "caboose" (an unexpected late-in-life baby).

I have rated each party theme's formality (♥), cost ($), and stress (!) level on a scale of one to five, with five being the highest. However, please don't let these ratings intimidate you, because you can always ask for help from family or friends. For example, if it will be a very expensive affair, such as a formal sit-down dinner, you may want to enlist several co-hosts who are able to help out with the costs. Likewise, if a certain party theme involves a lot of complicated planning and "doing," you may want to lower the stress factor by delegating some of the duties.

As you choose your theme, the main thing to keep in mind is to plan a memorable, entertaining shower—one your guests will remember fondly. I think we've all attended enough boring baby showers—the type of party where the only entertainment is watching the mother-to-be open gifts. It's time for a fun baby shower with a clever new theme, an unusual location, and a little creativity when it comes to the games, entertainment, and cuisine!

I'm sure you'll find the perfect theme for your party here; one that suits the expectant parents, the guests, and your own personal hostess profile. After all, you want to enjoy the party, too!

Chapter 1

All in the Family

A family party is usually more warm, fuzzy, and intimate than a traditional baby shower, and understandably so. After all, the couple's family members are the most important people in their lives and no one could be happier about the new addition to the family.

Family parties tend to be more relaxed and easier to plan. This chapter includes the Announcement Party, the Potluck Picnic Baby Shower, and the Family Heirloom Shower.

Announcement Party

> Formality - ♥ ♥
>
> Cost - $ $
>
> Stress - ! !

An announcement party is one where the couple announces for the first time that they are expecting a baby. It can be a surprise party, or it can be a party "tacked on" to the end of some other event, such as a Thanksgiving Day get-together, family Christmas party, or a birthday party. Of course, this party will not involve the giving of gifts to the expectant parents. The purpose at this point is to announce the pregnancy; a traditional shower can be planned for a later time.

The announcement itself may be made by the expectant father or by the grandfather-to-be, or it may be hidden inside a party favor. For example:

♦ On a small piece of paper folded and placed between two halves of a walnut shell, tied together with a narrow ribbon.

♦ On a long, narrow piece of paper that has been wrapped tightly around the stem of a silk or fresh flower.

♦ Inside a "cracker" favor (see Chp. 8).

Potluck Picnic Baby Shower

Formality -

Cost - $

Stress - !

If the couple comes from large families and there will be quite a crowd at your party, why not make it a good old-fashioned potluck picnic? That way you'll have plenty of room for everyone and there will be very little expense involved. You can reserve a designated area in a local park, rent a private park, or hold it at a family member's backyard if anyone in the family happens to live on a sizable piece of land.

Tie balloon bouquets to the ends of the picnic tables and place the gifts in large decorated laundry baskets. Set the tables with the usual red and white checkered tablecloths, bring several ice chests full of drinks, and let the fun begin.

You might want to play one or two old-fashioned Sunday school or Fourth of July picnic games, which are fun for everyone, especially great-aunts and -uncles, grandparents, and any other older folks who remember them with fondness.

For example, you could include a few of these favorites:

◆ Nail-pounding contest.

◆ Horseshoe competition.

◆ Egg toss or water balloon toss.

◆ Sack race.

◆ Three-legged race.

◆ Wheelbarrow race.

◆ Kick-the-shoe contest.

Note: See the "Family Shower" invitation in Chapter 7 and the "family tree" pattern in the Appendix.

Family Heirloom Shower

> **Formality - ♥ ♥ ♥**
>
> **Cost - $ $**
>
> **Stress - ! !**

This is a party for the female family members, and the theme of the party is to pass down family heirlooms or antiques in honor of the new baby. The type of heirlooms that are often passed down from generation to generation are:

◆ A christening dress.

◆ A hand-knitted or crocheted blanket.

◆ Silver baby spoon.

◆ Music box.

◆ Silver haircut box (to hold hair from first haircut).

◆ Silver tooth-fairy box.

◆ Silver or porcelain picture frames.

You can use the "Family Tree" pattern for your invitations and place cards and a small tree as your centerpiece (see Chp. 8).

For entertainment, here is one time where your guests won't be bored with home movies or family videos. Round up all the baby photos, home movies, and videotapes you can find of family members when they were young, especially those of the expectant parents. It will be fun to hear an aunt's or grandmother's story about some of the humorous things they remember about the mommy- or daddy-to-be as they were growing up.

As for the food, you can serve an informal luncheon buffet or an elegant tea party (see Chp. 12).

Tip: In addition to viewing home movies, family members may enjoy predicting the new baby's physical characteristics, such as Grandma's dimples or Uncle Fred's freckles, etc. Supply 3 x 5 cards and ask each family member to predict at least one of the baby's characteristics.

See Chapter 4 for more themes suitable for family showers.

Chapter 2

Just Us Girls

This chapter offers popular party themes suitable for a women-only baby shower. They range from an informal "Good-as-New Party" to a very formal "Alice in Wonderland Tea Party." I'm sure you'll find one that suits your time, talents, and budget.

Teddy Bear Shower

Formality - ♥ ♥

Cost - $ $

Stress - ! !

This is a low-stress party to put together because it's easy to round up teddy bears to use as decorations. Ask around and gather up as many teddy bears as you can find. Tie bows around their necks and balloons around their wrists and spread them around the room—in groups on the floor, in baskets, on tables, in a rocking chair, a bassinet, stroller, cradle, and so forth. Create a "Three Bears" centerpiece for your serving or gift table (see Chp. 8).

Tiny teddies can also be used to decorate the cake and teddy bear stickers can be added to the name tags and place cards. You can mail or hand deliver actual teddy bears with invitations attached, or you can customize your invitations by using the pattern provided in the Appendix.

If you can't come up with enough teddy bears to carry out your theme, use whatever you can find; any stuffed animals will work.

Tip: Put diapers on your animals with big diaper pins.

Sugar Plum Tree Shower

> Formality - ♥ ♥
>
> Cost - $ $
>
> Stress - ! !

This is another easy theme to work with because everything is candy-related. See Chapter 8 for decorating ideas, including a sugar plum tree centerpiece, tall "candy cane" decorations, and lollipop name tags and favors. There is also a sugar plum tree gift display described in Chapter 10.

Raggedy Ann and Andy Party

> Formality - ♥ ♥
>
> Cost - $ $
>
> Stress - ! !

This is similar to the teddy bear theme, except that you decorate with Raggedy Ann and Andy dolls. Incorporate the theme with the use of Raggedy Ann and Andy stickers, as well as frosting decoration on the cake.

If you can't come up with any of these dolls, you can use Disney Babies, Sesame Street characters, or Muppet Babies as your theme. If you don't want to make your own invitations and decorations for these alternative themes, you'll find that most of these characters are already available on coordinated invitations, paper plates, cups, napkins, and decorations.

Choo-Choo Train Party

Formality - ♥ ♥

Cost - $ $

Stress - ! !

Not only is a train theme perfect for a Caboose Shower (see Chp. 5), but it also works well for a baby boy, whether he has already been born or not.

Use the train pattern in the Appendix to create homemade invitations, place cards, name tags, and cake decorations. An electric train can serve as the table centerpiece or it can run on tracks that have been creatively placed in and around the platters of food on the buffet table. Or if you can't round up an electric train, create your own train by connecting boxes of animal crackers together with yarn.

Tip: Wear an engineer's cap and use a wooden train whistle as you conduct the games.

"Yes, You Can!" Shower

Formality - ♥

Cost - $ $

Stress - ! !

This shower theme works well when most of the guests are moms who are willing to share their advice. The idea is to ask guests to bring recipe cards offering their best advice for bringing up baby. Of course, you'll want to provide an attractive recipe box to hold the cards and present to the guest of honor at the end of the party.

Be sure to enclose a couple of index cards with each shower invitation, along with suggestions for the type of advice that will be appreciated by the mother-to-be. Here are a few ideas:

- ◆ Creative finger foods for toddlers.
- ◆ Homemade toys.
- ◆ Coping with motherhood.

Encourage your guests to decorate their cards and sign and date them.

Tip: As light entertainment during the party, you may want to read these cards out loud.

Good-as-New Party

> **Formality -** ♥
>
> **Cost -** $
>
> **Stress -** !

This is a casual, informal get-together where the expectant mom is "showered" with practical, quality used baby things, including clothing, blankets, crib quilts, bed pads, crib sheets, baby towels and wash cloths, plus larger items such as a stroller, high chair, baby swing, and so forth. So that there is no misunderstanding on the part of the mommy-to-be, be sure to explain the theme to her before the invitations go out.

Obviously, this is one of the least expensive and least stressful parties to host, not only for you, but for the guests. Suggest that your guests shop at garage sales and thrift stores. However, even though the gifts may be "hand-me-downs," a party is still in order, complete with decorations, games, and refreshments.

Tip: The gifts can be wrapped in new "designer" diapers. That way, the mommy-to-be will receive a dozen or so new diapers in addition to the second-hand gifts.

Pamper Mommy Party

Formality - ♥

Cost - $ $ / $ $ $

Stress - ! !

This is a party in honor of the expectant mother, as opposed to one that honors the arrival of the new baby. The idea is to pamper the mommy-to-be by giving her personal items that she can use in the hospital or at home after the baby is born.

Anyone who has never been pregnant probably won't have any idea what I'm talking about, but by the time the due date rolls around, the novelty of being an expectant mother has warn off. No more "You're so beautiful when you're pregnant" remarks, or "Isn't this the most precious thing?" comments from the family. Instead, by this time the poor mother-to-be not only feels fat and "swollen," but she has a cracking backache!

This brings us to our "Pamper Mommy Party." You can begin with a free makeover, compliments of your favorite cosmetics representative, followed by the services of a professional manicurist or a hair stylist who will create a fresh new look for the guest of honor.

Guests may want to give individual gifts, such as a lacy, feminine nightie, a satin robe and slippers, a bed jacket, or a nice group gift such as a basket filled with such things as bath powder, lotions, perfume, books, magazines, and a couple of her favorite candy bars.

Fill-The-Freezer Shower

Formality - ♥ ♥

Cost - $ $

Stress - ! !

This is a great idea for the mother who is expecting her second or third child, because she probably has all the basics and what she *really* needs is some relief during the first two or three weeks after the baby is born. So, what could be better than to furnish her with frozen homemade casseroles, desserts, breads, etc.?

In addition to the frozen dishes, each guest is asked to bring the corresponding recipe written out on a 3 x 5 card, which is then placed in an attractive photo album to be given to the guest of honor at the end of the party. That way, if her family really loves the dish, she'll know how to make it again and, meanwhile, the prepared meals will keep her out of the kitchen, freeing her up to spend time with her new baby, as well as her older children.

Gift Certificate Shower

Formality - ♥

Cost - $ $

Stress - !

This is a party where the guests bring gift certificates good for such things as:

♦ One free evening of baby-sitting.

♦ One complete dinner, delivered to your door.

♦ A gift certificate good for one free pie or cake per month for a year.

♦ Free hours of running errands.

♦ A month of chauffeuring duties (for any older children who need rides to/from school, sports practice, etc.).

♦ "First Night on the Town"—a group gift that includes several gift certificates, such as:

⇨ One free evening of baby-sitting.

⇨ Corsage and boutonniere from a local florist.

⇨ Dinner for two at a fine restaurant.

⇨ Movie, concert, or theater tickets.

Believe me, a new mother will appreciate every single gift certificate she receives!

So that all the certificates will be uniform, you can duplicate the gift certificate below to be enclosed with the party invitations.

Gift Certificate

Good for:

_____

From:

_____

Time-of-Day Shower

Formality - ♥ ♥

Cost - $ $

Stress - ! !

The theme of this party is time, so when you prepare the party invitations, assign a specific time of day to each guest, with a request to bring a baby gift that can be used accordingly. For example:

- Bath time (9 a.m.): bath thermometer.
- Lunch time (noon): tipper cup.
- Nap time (2 p.m.): sleepers.
- Play time (4 p.m.): stuffed animals.

A grandfather clock can be decorated with ribbons and baby-related items to serve as the main party decoration, and the clock theme can also be carried through on the invitations, name tags, place cards, and cake. Toy wrist watches can be used as favors.

Dolly Shower

Formality - ♥ ♥

Cost - $ $

Stress - ! !

The theme is "dolls, dolls, and more dolls." Create a display of valuable antique dolls, such as Madame Alexander dolls, or fill a cradle, bassinet, or child's rocking chair with baby dolls or Barbie dolls. You can also use toy nursery furniture, including a crib, stroller, high chair, etc., all filled with dolls. Attach miniature plastic babies to the name tags or place cards, and serve Barbie Doll Cake or Ice Cream Babies (see Chp. 14).

Alice in Wonderland Tea Party

Formality - ♥ ♥ ♥ ♥ ♥

Cost - $ $ $ $

Stress - ! ! ! !

Although this is a light-hearted theme, it is still a formal affair. Lay your table out with linen and lace, setting a delicate centerpiece of violets and baby's breath and placing simple nosegays at each place setting.

Any of the Alice in Wonderland characters can be used to inspire your decorations, including Alice, the Mad Hatter, Dormouse, March Hare, Queen of Hearts, White Rabbit, or the Cheshire Cat. Go to the library and check out an illustrated copy of the book to get an idea of what they look like so you'll know how to dress up a stuffed white or brown rabbit, a doll to look like Alice, or a top hat to look like the Mad Hatter's. Have fun with this theme!

Mommy's Five-Star Treat

Formality - ♥ ♥ ♥

Cost - $ $ $ $ $

Stress - !

Whether the guest of honor is a first-time or second-time mom, why not pamper her with an elegant lunch at an upscale restaurant? This type of baby shower is a great idea for the hostess who doesn't have the time or energy to plan a complicated party. In fact, it is one of the least stressful ways to host a shower that everyone will appreciate.

Send elegant invitations that give the time, place, and purpose of the get-together. Guests may bring individual gifts or, especially in the case of a second-time mom, they might want to pool resources to purchase something she really needs for the baby but didn't receive the first time around, such as a bassinet, playpen, or a quality stroller. In fact, if the mom has other young children, she may appreciate a two-seat stroller so she can venture out and comfortably manage the new baby and a toddler.

Although the shower takes place in a restaurant, you can bring a floral centerpiece, favors, or place cards, all of which will personalize and "party up" the table, giving it a special touch.

Mother Goose Shower

Formality -

Cost - $ $ / $ $ $

Stress - !

This is a "participation party" where the guests come prepared to recite a nursery rhyme or sing a lullaby to the baby—on tape, of course. Use the Nursery Rhyme shower invitation suggested in Chapter 7 to let the guests know what to expect.

In lieu of games or entertainment, the highlight of this shower is the "recording session" where guests will take turns singing or reciting their selections onto a cassette tape. If this recording session gets a little silly, or if the guests ham things up, all the better. The tape will become a treasured memento of the party and—who knows?—it may actually entertain the baby as he or she is growing up!

Be sure to encourage guests to bring their own musical accompaniment if they would like. Also, let them know that original compositions will receive special recognition. (Have extra-special prizes on hand for any guests who come prepared with something they have composed themselves.) You may need to round up a good quality tape recorder, preferably with a microphone, and be sure to have plenty of blank tapes on hand.

If you're asked for gift ideas, you may want to suggest decorative items that relate to nursery rhymes, such as a lamp, posters, pillows, crib mobile, night light, or a music box.

By the way, be sure to have a few nursery rhymes or Dr. Seuss books on hand for guests who arrive unprepared.

Stork Shower

Formality - ♥ ♥

Cost - $ $

Stress - ! !

Finally, we come to the all-time favorite: a stork shower. This is another one of those themes that's easy to put together because stork-related decorations are readily available at party supply stores. Use the stork pattern in the Appendix for the invitations, name tags, and place cards, as well as for the cake.

You'll find affordable fold-out stork centerpieces for sale in party-supply stores, and you can rent a stork for your front yard (see Chp. 8).

Tip: After all the guests have arrived, bring the stork inside to "watch over" the gifts.

Other baby shower themes appropriate for a women-only shower include:

- A specific baby gift theme ("Baby Clothes," "Baby Toys," "Furnish the Nursery," etc.).
- Cradles.
- Umbrellas.
- Clowns.
- Baby's carousel.
- Rocking horses.
- Quilting bee.
- Littlest angel.
- Country Garden Party (Chp. 4).
- "Little Cowboy" or "Little Cowgirl" Barbecue (Chp. 4).
- "You Must Have Been a Beautiful Baby" Party (Chp. 4).
- Hawaiian Luau (Chp. 4).
- A "Room-for-Baby" Party (Chp. 4).
- Everyone's Expecting (Chp. 4).
- Holiday Baby Shower (Chp. 4).
- Potluck Picnic (Chp. 1).

Chapter 3

Where the Boys Are

Baby showers have traditionally been given for the expectant mother, but a first-time daddy appreciates a party, too—after all, he *did* have something to do with this whole thing. One of these parties is a casual get-together sans decorations and games. It may be as simple as an extended coffee break where his co-workers present him with gifts, or a planned evening of "male bonding" hosted by friends—one last hurrah before moving on to midnight feedings and diaper changing. Unlike a conventional baby shower, a "Daddy Party" doesn't need a theme *per se*, but here are a few ways to give it a little personality.

A "Roast"

Formality - ♥

Cost - $ $ $

Stress - ! ! !

A roast usually follows a sit-down dinner, whether it takes place in a side room of your favorite restaurant or it's a catered meal in someone's home. The idea is to have a speaker's stand, called a "dais," located at one of the tables. The men take turns telling stories about the daddy-to-be, "roasting" him by recounting the dumbest or most embarrassing things he's ever done.

The key to the success of one of these parties is to be careful that you don't reveal anything *too* personal or humiliating. Also, be sure to end your roast on a sincere note, telling why the guest of honor will make such a terrific father.

Men's Night Out

Formality -

Cost - $ $ $

Stress - !

Make plans to attend a macho movie, a boxing match, a live concert, or a performance of a favorite comedian at a local comedy club. If this idea seems a little pricey to you, you can always rent a movie or a live concert on video tape, or watch a pay-per-view boxing match in your own family room.

Another affordable option is an informal poker party, or any other card game. Whether a rousing "Hearts" tournament or winner-take-all poker game, the men will enjoy the bonding and camaraderie. Just be sure you have plenty of food and drink on hand, along with a box of fine cigars. Set up a table loaded with cold meats, cheeses, breads, condiments, chips and dips, pretzels, and mixed nuts, along with drinks and plenty of ice. The important thing is that all the foods can be eaten with the hands so the guys won't have to juggle plates and silverware during the competition.

Tip: There's nothing like a night of male bonding to whet a man's appetite, so provide twice as much food as you think they'll eat—and it will probably be just right!

Sports Participation Party

Formality -

Cost - $ $

Stress - !

An active sports-oriented get-together is another popular trend—in part because it provides the expectant father a way to blow off a little steam. After all, the *waiting*, especially during that last month or so before the baby arrives, can be pretty stressful, and physical activity may provide a good outlet for the stress.

Whatever sport you choose, make it even more fun by providing prizes or trophies for first, second, and third place. In the case of a golf tournament, for example, you could give out prizes for "Closest to the Hole" or "Longest Drive," and so forth.

To top it all off, be sure you've made plans to eat together after the big event, whether it's just a hamburger in the clubhouse after golf or tennis, a stop at a diner on the way home, or a barbecue beside the water at the end of a day of fishing or rafting.

Oh, by the way, in addition to the gifts, don't forget to bring along a box of quality cigars. After all, cigar smoking *is* the latest trend in male bonding!

Here are a few popular sports to consider:

- Tennis.
- Golf.
- Volleyball.
- Horseshoes.
- Bicycle marathon.
- Bowling.
- Pool or billiards.
- Camping or backpacking.
- Rafting.
- Snow or water skiing.
- Snowmobiling.
- Fishing.
- Racquetball or handball.
- Any other sport of your choice!

Tailgate Party

> **Formality -**
>
> **Cost - $ $/$ $ $**
>
> **Stress - !**

Buy box seat tickets and have the guys bring their gloves to a professional baseball game, or, depending on the season, round up tickets to watch your favorite football, basketball, or hockey team play a home game. Of course, by watching instead of participating, the guys won't get in as much physical activity, but it can still be a great time together.

Other themes suitable for a men-only shower:

♦ A "Room-for-Baby" Party (Chp. 4).
♦ Like Father, Like Son Shower (Chp. 4).
♦ Office Party (Chp. 5).

Tip: See "Gifts for Daddy" suggestions in Chapter 10.

Chapter 4

Co-ed Parties

The key to a successful co-ed baby shower is to forget about "shower" and think in terms of "party." Whether a formal or informal affair, the goal should be for everyone to have a good time.

This chapter includes three lovely formal affairs and eight creative informal party themes.

FORMAL PARTIES

Elegant Sit-Down Dinner

Formality - ♥ ♥ ♥ ♥ ♥

Cost - $ $ $ $ $

Stress - ! ! ! ! !

The menu for a formal sit-down dinner is usually quite elaborate and served plate service or French service (see Chp. 12). And because the meal is so elaborate and has so many courses, it takes up most of the evening. Therefore, the party becomes a talk party, as opposed to a game party.

In addition, you may decide to engage the services of professional musicians to perform during the meal service, such as a stringed trio, or, if you really want to impress your guests as they enjoy their after-dinner coffee, arrange for a soloist or instrumentalist to present a mini-concert.

Look in Chapter 8 for centerpiece and table decoration ideas, including napkin folding and place cards.

The evening culminates, of course, with the opening of the gifts.

Candlelight Dessert Party

Formality - ♥ ♥ ♥ ♥

Cost - $ $ $

Stress - ! ! !

This is an excellent choice if you would like to host a formal party, but you don't have the time or funds to plan a sit-down dinner. The ambience is created with candles, fresh or silk pink roses, and lots of swirling tulle netting and delicate pink and blue ribbons. You can add a little more light, as well, by stringing tiny all-white Christmas lights along the tables, around the plants or garlands, and over doorways. This theme works best, of course, as an evening affair.

In addition to your own personal favorites, you'll find several popular dessert recipes in Chapter 14. Because this is a formal party, you may want to limit the entertainment to soft background music, good conversation, and, of course, the opening of the gifts.

If you like the idea of a dessert party, but you would like to host one that is less formal, you can use less elaborate decorations and include any of the games or activities described in Chapter 9.

Country Garden Party

> Formality - ♥ ♥ ♥ ♥
>
> Cost - $ $ $
>
> Stress - ! ! !

A country garden party works best outdoors in an actual garden setting. If it is held indoors, however, you can still create the illusion of a garden by decorating with pots of real and artificial flowers, silk ficus trees, park benches, birdbaths filled with floating candles and gardenias, a white trellis entwined with paper flowers, a low white picket fence, and patio tables with umbrellas set with potted geraniums. Reserve one table for the gifts.

You can serve tea sandwiches and salads or a luncheon buffet (see Chp. 12).

INFORMAL PARTIES

"Little Cowboy" or "Cowgirl" Barbecue

> Formality -
>
> Cost - $ $ $ $
>
> Stress - ! ! !

Drag out your cowboy boots, 10-gallon hats, and bandannas for this party, and encourage your guests to get into the spirit by wearing their western outfits too. Make a centerpiece out of a cowboy hat, turned upside down and filled with a container of flowers or a plant.

Decorate with cowboy hats, saddles, branding irons, singletrees, potted cactus plants, hay bales and red-checkered tablecloths. Use the cowboy hat pattern in the Appendix for the invitations and name tags.

See the Little Cowboy or Cowgirl Barbecue menu in Chapter 12.

Tip: A rocking horse makes a nice group gift from the hosts.

"You Must Have Been a Beautiful Baby" Party

> **Formality - ♥ ♥**
>
> **Cost - $ $ $**
>
> **Stress - ! !**

Collect as many of the couple's baby photos as you can, along with home movies or videotapes, plus the couple's own teddy bears, if they still exist, to be used as decorations.

The main entertainment consists of "Show and Tell," where the photos are passed around for all to see, along with home movies or videos of the mommy- and daddy-to-be when they were growing up.

You can serve party snacks and finger foods (see Chp. 11), desserts (see Chp. 14), or an informal meal (see Chp. 12).

Hawaiian Luau

> **Formality - ♥ ♥**
>
> **Cost - $ $ $ $**
>
> **Stress - ! ! ! !**

A luau is an easy party to organize; all you need are a few tiki torches, grass skirts, ukuleles, and flower leis, plus, if you happen to have a pool, a floating raft filled with bright paper, or fresh flowers. This is a "hang loose," relaxed party, so do everything you can to make the guests feel comfortable: Wear a Hawaiian sarong or shirt, furnish the guests with fresh flower or synthetic leis, and have plenty of soothing Hawaiian music playing in the background.

Of course, the success of a luau depends on the quality of the food and the way it's presented. A complete luau menu is provided in Chapter 12.

A "Room-for-Baby" Party

Formality -

Cost - $ $ / $ $ $

Stress - !

This is a "work party" that takes place at the couple's home, so you'll obviously need to consult with the expectant parents ahead of time. Guests should arrive in their "work grubbies" and pitch in to help the couple paint, wallpaper, or decorate the baby's room. Bring any tools you'll need, such as paint brushes or wallpapering gear. In addition to the tools, the guests are asked to bring casseroles, salads, desserts, and drinks for the party that follows. The guests' gifts are in the form of their elbow grease, plus any materials they would like to contribute to the cause, such as paint, wallpaper, decorations, or items for the baby's room.

As host or hostess, all you'll need to furnish are a few simple decorations, plus disposable tablecloths, tableware, trash bags, and plenty of extra ice.

Tip: You can always order pizza for delivery at quitting time.

"And Daddy Too" Shower

Formality - ♥

Cost - $ $ $

Stress - ! ! !

The concept of this party is really very simple: It is a baby shower for the expectant mother where the daddy-to-be, spouses of the women guests, plus other male relatives arrive *after* the gifts have been opened and just in time for the most important element of the party: the food!

This idea works best when there is something fun for the guys to do during the first part of the shower, such as watching a sporting event on TV in another room, playing a game of volley ball or horseshoes in the back yard, or watching a boxing match on cable, an action flick at a theater, or a video rented for the occasion.

Since the food is the main attraction for the men, you may want to try one of "Paul Bunyan's Hearty Favorites" described in Chapter 12, such as Blue Ox Reubens or Hungry Man's Hamburger Pie.

Everyone's Expecting

> Formality - ♥
>
> Cost - $ $
>
> Stress - !

This is a tongue-in-cheek type of party where all the guests, including the men, arrive *quite* "pregnant." The idea is "we sympathize with you, because we're all going through the same thing." Keep the idea a secret. It will be a great surprise to the expectant mother.

Tip: Suggest that the guests wear big shirts or borrowed maternity clothes over their puffy-pillow tummies. Give prizes for "The Funniest," "Most Creative," etc.

"Like Father Like Son" Shower

> Formality - ♥
>
> Cost - $ $
>
> Stress - ! !

This theme works best when the expectant parents know the sex of the baby. The idea is to plan the party around the mother's or father's profession. For example, if the father is in law enforcement, they may be expecting a "junior police cadet." Other ideas include a junior fireman, an apprentice realtor, assistant professor, and so forth.

Carry the theme all the way through from the invitations to the cake by decorating with toy police cars, fire engines, houses with "For Sale" signs out in front, etc.

Block Party

> Formality -
>
> Cost - $
>
> Stress - !

Here's a terrific idea for a casual neighborhood baby shower. Plan a potluck block party with barbecued hamburgers and hot dogs, along with salads, drinks, and a cake.

Invite everyone by word-of-mouth or over the telephone. Of course, no name tags or place cards will be required, so all you'll need to furnish are the cake and a few helium balloons.

Tip: Be sure to provide a sturdy, comfortable patio chair for the expectant mama, plus something to hold the gifts, such as a decorated wheelbarrow or child's wagon.

Holiday Baby Showers

> Formality - ♥ ♥
>
> Cost - $ $ / $ $ $
>
> Stress - ! ! !

Build your theme around a holiday that is close to the baby's due date or the party date. A holiday theme is easy to work with because decorations are so readily available. Here are a few holiday ideas:

New Year's Baby Shower

Treat this party as a celebration of the baby's upcoming birth. Use New Year's Eve party props, such as party horns, party hats, confetti, and champagne to welcome the new baby and the new year.

Tip: Be sure to have nonalcoholic champagne on hand for the mommy-to-be and the teetotalers.

Valentine's Baby Shower

What could be more appropriate than hearts and baby Cupids? Place a baby doll on a heart-shaped pillow as a table centerpiece and serve heart-shaped sugar cookies. Use children's valentines as favors or place cards and fashion a giant red heart valentine that says "We Love You Baby _____" to stand beside the gift display.

For fun, ask everyone to guess the number of candy hearts in a clear glass fish bowl. The guest who comes closest receives the candy-filled bowl as a prize.

St. Patrick's Day Baby Shower

Just think "green and white" for this party—everything from the balloons to the streamers to the food. Serve shamrock-shaped sugar cookies with lime sherbet for dessert or Blarney Stone Cobbler (see Chp. 14), along with Irish Coffee (see Chp. 13).

Easter Baby Shower

Let Easter eggs be your theme for this pastel-colored shower. Decorate with pink, yellow, and blue balloons and plastic eggs filled with candy or marshmallow bunnies. Set tiny decorated Easter baskets at the place settings as favors, and a larger basket filled with plastic grass and stuffed bunnies as a table centerpiece. Or you can use the idea given in Chapter 9 for an egg centerpiece (a giant egg with a baby peeking out).

Tip: Blooming tulips and daffodils will add color to the room.

Fourth of July Baby Shower

Splash the party site with plenty of red, white, and blue—from balloons to streamers to American flags. A mini-fireworks display will serve as entertainment and for dessert serve a cake covered with tiny flags.

Tip: If you really want to impress your guests, turn the lights off and carry in the cake with lighted sparklers on top.

Christmas Baby Shower

The month of December is the easiest time of all to host a shower because you can take advantage of the decorations you already have on display in your home. However, you may want to add a few more angels than usual. Place the shower gifts under the Christmas tree and serve traditional Christmas fare, plus a Wonderful Wassail Bowl, Christmas Baby Punch, or Humpty Dumpty's Nog (see Chp. 13).

After gifts have been opened and refreshments have been served, top off the evening with a caroling parade around the neighborhood.

Other holiday possibilities include:

◆ Chinese New Year.
◆ Mardi Gras.
◆ Cinco de Mayo.
◆ Memorial Day.
◆ Halloween.
◆ Hanukkah.
◆ Kwanzaa.

Other themes suitable for a co-ed shower include:

◆ Gift Certificate Shower (Chp. 2).
◆ Tailgate Party (Chp. 3).

Chapter 5

Specialty Parties

Special circumstances—such as twins, absentee parents, adoptions, and "caboose" babies—often provide ideas for creative themes. Here are examples of some typical situations.

Twice as Nice!

Formality - ♥ ♥

Cost - $ $

Stress - ! ! !

If the mommy- and daddy-to-be are expecting twins, your theme will be easy to incorporate into your party because everything will be in twos.

For example, you can use twin babies for your invitations, name tags, place cards, and as a pattern for the top of the cake. You can decorate using two dolls sitting together in a doll stroller, crib, or bassinet, two teddy bears sitting side by side with their arms around each other, and so forth.

The gift display may consist of two umbrellas tied together with ribbons. Write the babies' names on two helium balloons and tie them together. Place them at the end of the serving table, beside the guest of honor's chair, or by the front door.

Tip: Be sure to embellish Mommy's corsage with two sets of baby booties, two baby rattles, two miniature baby bottles, etc.

Long-Distance Baby Shower

Formality - ♥ ♥

Cost - $ $ $

Stress - ! !

This is a shower that takes place for absentee parents, such as a couple who recently moved away to another city or state, or perhaps a couple doing military or mission work in another country.

The object of this party is to include the expectant parents in everything that's going on—from the games, to the gift-giving, to the eats. The gifts are brought to the party unwrapped so that everyone can see them. They are wrapped during the party as one of the activities and shipped by the hostess at a later date.

The expectant parents can be included in the party in a number of ways:

- ♦ Through an open telephone line to the couple during the party itself.
- ♦ By taking photos during the party, to be included with the gifts when they are sent.
- ♦ By passing around a blank book during the party with the request that each guest write a personal message to the expectant parents. The book is enclosed with the gifts.
- ♦ By videotaping the party, including a personal message from each guest. The guests should also be encouraged to tell humorous stories about the raising of children or, in the case of the couple's relatives, incidents that happened when the expectant parents were babies or toddlers.

Be sure to videotape the refreshment time, as well, promising to send along samples with the gifts. Obviously, you'll need to serve a dessert that will travel well, such as brownies or cookies.

Tip: Suggest gifts that are easy to mail—nothing fragile.

Portable Party

Formality - ♥

Cost - $ $

Stress - ! !

If you're too busy to plan a traditional shower, you can always bring the party to the guests of honor. If the expectant parents sing in the church choir, for example, why not spring a party on them after a choir practice? Or if she is a member of the Great Books Club, you could bring refreshments and a balloon bouquet to one of their meetings as a surprise. Or you can even drop in on her at her own home, as long as her husband is in on the plans.

Another popular idea is to prepare simple "brown bag" lunches for everyone that can be taken to the park for an impromptu picnic. The bags can be pink or blue or white—and you can decorate them if you have time with baby-related stickers or other decorations.

Of course, the guests will need to know about the party ahead of time! After all, they'll want to help shower her with gifts for the new baby.

First-Time Grandma or Grandpa

Formality - ♥

Cost - $ $

Stress - ! !

Grandma and Grandpa are excited, too—especially if this is their first grandchild! So, plan a special party just for him or her, complete with gifts chosen especially with the grandparent in mind, such as a baby photo brag book, disposable diapers, pacifiers, or even a comfortable rocking chair.

An appropriate group gift would be a "Grandparent Emergency Kit"—a basket filled with all those little things that are so important when the new grandchild visits, such as baby powder, baby soaps and shampoo, baby lotion, diaper rash ointment, diaper pins, teething ring, baby rattles, receiving blankets and, of course, a cuddly teddy bear.

Each guest may want to contribute something to this basket, or everyone may decide to go together on one expensive gift, such as a crib or a playpen.

There are also many clever personal gifts on the market, such as T-shirts that say "Foxy Grandma," for example, or bumper stickers and license plate frames that say things such as "Happiness is Being a Grandparent."

Office Party

Formality - ♥

Cost - $ $

Stress - ! !

An office party takes very little in the way of planning, decorating, and expense—it's the thought that counts! Set out extra-special bakery treats in one of the meeting rooms or in someone's office, decorate with a simple balloon bouquet, and invite the mommy- or daddy-to-be for an extended coffee break. It doesn't get much easier than that!

Another option is to bring the party to a nearby restaurant where everyone can order their lunch "Dutch treat." Or how about ordering box lunches from a local deli that can be carried to a nearby park?

Invitations can be created in the form of office memos, with clever wording such as, "Come See What Karen Has Been Up To

Lately" or "Come Meet Marketing's New Cheerleader," and so forth. See Chapter 7 for an example of an Office Memo invitation.

Everyone can bring an individual gift for the baby or you can take up a collection to purchase something major for the nursery, such as a crib or bassinet. One popular twist on the latter is to gift wrap a box containing a *photograph* of the gift that has been cut into 20 or so pieces, forming a jigsaw puzzle. The guest of honor works with the pieces until he or she identifies the gift. The actual gift is delivered to the home, which is nice because the guest of honor won't have to transport it.

To tell the truth, anything you plan is guaranteed to be a success because *everyone* would rather party than work!

Adopted Baby Celebration

Formality - ♥ ♥

Cost - $ $

Stress - ! ! !

An adopted child is a very special little person who deserves a very special party! In fact, the shower evolves way beyond a mere party and becomes a joyous celebration.

Not only do the parents need all the same paraphernalia as any parent would, but they also need the love and support of their friends and family.

The decision to pursue adoption is monumental in itself, but the adoption process is even more so. First comes the paperwork, then the legalities, the financial obligations, and the angst of the waiting. When Mommy and Daddy finally hold their child in their arms, their joy is beyond words.

So, as you plan the shower, try to make it a celebration that's as festive as possible. You can drape banners inside and out that say "Welcome Ashley," for example. And you can use that same slogan on the invitations, name tags, place cards, favors, and the cake.

....

By the way, when it comes to the cake, how about a "lighted sparklers presentation" to add to the celebration!

Tip: During the party, it's a good idea to refer to the baby as the "new baby," *not* the "adopted baby."

Caboose Shower

Formality - ♥ ♥

Cost - $ $

Stress - ! !

A caboose shower is hosted in honor of parents who are expecting a "caboose baby"—long after the births of their other children. For example, a couple may have two married children and already be grandparents when along comes a surprise—a little caboose baby at the end of the train!

Use the "caboose" idea as your theme, from the invitations to the place cards to the table centerpiece, which can be an electric train that has a decorated caboose with a tiny baby on board—looking out a window or propped behind the railing at the end of the caboose.

Decorate your cake with a miniature train, including cars that have the names of the other children if you would like. This will make them feel part of the celebration, too!

See the Appendix for a train pattern.

Part II

Planning the Party

Now that you've chosen a theme, you're ready to plan the party. In addition to anything you might need to customize the party for your theme, here are the basic factors to consider when planning a baby shower:

♦ Choosing a location.
♦ Selecting the right invitation.
♦ Finding the perfect decorations.
♦ Choosing perfect games and entertainment.
♦ Selecting gifts and prizes.

As you consider the various options, keep your theme in mind, adopting those ideas that not only fit in with your theme, but your budget and time constraints, as well. To simplify your planning, be sure to use the to-do lists, scheduler, and money minder in Chapters 15, 16, and 17.

Chapter 6

Choosing the Location

The traditional baby shower has usually been held in someone's home. Today's baby showers have broken with tradition, however, and may be held anywhere—at the office, during a club meeting, in a restaurant, or at a public park.

One of the reasons for this is that the father-to-be is often invited to the party. And, of course, there are more and more parties hosted exclusively for the expectant father, which is as it should be.

CONSIDERATIONS FOR SELECTING A LOCATION

Number of guests. The first consideration is the number of guests. If you're inviting less than 12 to 15 women to a traditional baby shower, your living room will probably be just the right size. But if you're inviting a dozen or more couples, especially if you'll be serving a meal from a buffet table, you may need a larger facility.

Party budget. Some locations are more affordable than others. Of course, a private home is the least expensive option, but there are also affordable sites for a larger party, such as a church hall, your country club, or a conference room at work.

Party theme and menu. The party's theme and menu will also dictate the party's location. For example, if you're planning a Hawaiian luau, a large backyard with a swimming pool would be an ideal location; or, if you're planning a potluck family picnic, you'll need a park-like setting.

Who will provide the food? Many sites require you to use their catering services, in addition to parking valets, coat attendants, bartenders, etc. If this is what you want, fine. However, if you would like to furnish some or all of the food and drink yourself, or you would like to bring in an outside caterer, you will need to book a site that allows you to do so. Here's a list of less expensive sites that allow you to have full control. Choosing one of these locations will not only save you money on the site itself, but on the per-person cost of the food as well.

- Private home.
- Country club.
- Church hall.
- Club meeting room.
- Restaurant.
- Office meeting room.
- Public park.
- Clubhouse or party room belonging to a gated, retirement, or apartment complex.

You will find a fill-in-the-blanks party site planning sheet in Chapter 16.

Chapter 7

Selecting the Right Invitation

Once you know what type of party you're going to host and where it will be held, you'll obviously need to invite the guests. The invitations may be formal or informal, engraved or homemade. But before we get into that, let's discuss some basic issues.

PREPARING THE INVITATIONS

Who Should Be Invited?

The traditional baby shower has been a party for the mother-to-be where the guests have been her closest women friends and family members. However, times have changed, and as I mentioned in the Introduction, the trend is toward co-ed parties that honor the expectant parents together. It's nice to confer with the honored guest(s) for names, addresses, and telephone numbers of friends and relatives who should be invited.

Tip: If you decide to make it a co-ed party, it's usually a good idea to keep the male-female ratio roughly equal.

How Many Guests Should I Invite?

Depending on the party's theme and location, this number will usually vary between eight and 30. If you're hosting an elegant women-only tea party in your dining room, for example, you may invite only six or eight of the expectant mother's closest friends and immediate family members. However, if you're hosting a backyard barbecue where there's plenty of room and the theme lends itself to a larger crowd, you may decide to invite a dozen couples or more.

There's also the matter of money to consider; the more guests, the more the party will cost.

What Type of Invitation Is Best?

Depending on the theme and formality of your party, an invitation may be engraved, handwritten, homemade, or delivered by telephone, e-mail, or fax. One word of caution about telephone calls, though: because our lives have become so busy and complicated, it is probably best to follow up with something in writing. If you don't, you're taking the chance the person won't remember the correct date or time or, worse yet, that she'll forget the party altogether.

What Should Be Included on the Invitation?

Here is the basic information that the invitation should provide:

- ◆ Name of the guest(s) of honor.
- ◆ Name of the host(s).
- ◆ Date and time of the party.
- ◆ Location of the party with map or directions, if necessary. (Be sure to include the telephone number at the party location in case anyone gets lost.)
- ◆ Party's theme and dress code, if applicable.
- ◆ Suggested gift ideas, if applicable.
- ◆ Store where couple is registered.
- ◆ RSVP information (with a deadline for responding).

Here are some points to keep in mind as you decide the specific details of the party.

Let the expectant parent(s) set the actual date. Be sure to check with the guests of honor before you set the date to see when they are free. By checking with the expectant parents first, you may discover that they would feel more comfortable having the shower after the baby is born—just to be sure the child has arrived safely. And, of course, they may also like the idea of bringing their new baby to the party to show off the real guest of honor.

A shower given *after* the baby is born is nice for the hostess and guests, too, because everyone will know the sex and name of the baby, making it easier to plan the party and choose appropriate gifts. On the other hand, some expectant parents like the idea of a shower taking place before the baby arrives. That way the gifts will help stock the nursery in advance, and the parents will know what they still need to purchase before the big day.

Be sure the date doesn't conflict with another party. Call around to see if your date will conflict with any other parties being hosted for the couple.

Choose a date that is convenient for your guests. Give some thought to your guests' schedules; if most of them work Monday through Friday, a weekend party is probably best.

Choose an appropriate time of day. In choosing a time for the shower, consider what is best for your guest(s) of honor, as well as what is convenient for you. After all, you need plenty of time to clean, decorate, and prepare the food. Also, keep in mind the theme of the party and the type of food you will be serving.

List gift suggestions on the invitation, if appropriate. It's a good idea to find out what items the expectant parents have already purchased or received, as well as what they need. That way you can offer gift suggestions to the guests, either on the invitation itself, or by suggesting they call you. See Chapter 10 for gift suggestions.

Tell guests where the couple has registered. It has become a popular practice for expectant parents to register at a baby furnishings store. If the guests of honor have registered, be sure and note the information on the invitation; that way the couple will get things they really want and need, and duplication of gifts will be minimized.

Choosing Invitations

Here are a few suggestions for you to consider when choosing your invitations. I've divided them into three categories: Formal, Informal, and Novelty.

Formal Invitations

- An engraved or laser-printed invitation is best if the party will be a formal occasion, such as a sit-down dinner or a formal tea.
- If the invitations are computer-generated and laser-printed, be sure to use high quality card stock with a satin finish.
- For a very special touch, have elegant blank note cards handwritten by a calligrapher.

Informal Invitations

An informal invitation is suitable for most of the parties suggested in this book. You can:

- Purchase pre-printed invitations, choosing a style that comes closest to the theme of your party. If you do decide to use pre-printed invitations, however, you can add a special touch by hand writing a personalized note at the bottom of the invitation, such as, "We sure hope you can come to share Bob and Janette's happiness."
- Customize your invitations with an instant "personalizer machine" at a Hallmark store.
- Make your own.

Novelty Invitations

Some of these invitations may require hand delivery or extra postage if sent through the mail.

Baby diapers. Cut triangular pieces from stationery, construction paper or fabric. Fold into a tri-fold diaper, fastening with a safety pin or diaper pin. If a cloth diaper, the party invitation can be printed onto a triangular piece of paper that is inserted inside the diaper and is revealed when it is unpinned. If the diaper is created out of stationery or construction paper, you can print directly onto the inside of the diaper. The diapers can be inserted into square envelopes for mailing.

A diaper invitation will look something like this:

Teddy bears. You can purchase four-inch teddy bears for about a dollar a piece—the cutest I've seen for the money so far are available in the craft/fabric department at Wal-Mart. Tie ribbons around their necks, attach the invitations to the ribbons and hand deliver or mail in a small box.

You can also design your own teddy bear invitation using teddy bear stickers, clip art, or graphic art that may be available on your computer graphics program. Or you can use the teddy bear pattern in the Appendix by enlarging it so there is enough room to print the entire invitation on the bear's tummy.

Chocolate or bubble gum cigars. Write your party information on narrow tags that can be attached to the cigars. Tie the cigars with pink, blue, or yellow ribbons.

Paper dolls. Purchase a book of paper dolls. Cut out the dolls and their clothing. Write your party details on the outfits and enclose with one of the paper dolls.

Cowboy hats. Miniature cowboy hats with invitations tied at the brim. These hats can be purchased in the favors section at a party supply store, or you can use the pattern in the Appendix to create cowboy hats out of construction paper or heavy felt.

Babies. Purchase tiny babies wrapped in receiving blankets from a party supply store or your local dollar store. Attach the invitations to the babies' wrists (or pin them to the blankets). Or you can use the baby pattern in the Appendix to create invitations out of construction paper. If the couple is expecting twins or triplets, use two or three of these babies side by side.

Hawaiian leis. Attach a Hawaiian lei or shell necklace to the invitation. (Ask the guests to arrive at the party wearing their leis or necklaces.)

Plastic baby bottles. You can send full-size or toy baby bottles with the invitations tucked inside, or filled with gum drops with the invitation tied to the necks.

Holiday-related prop. Depending on the holiday theme of your party, you may want to send New Year's Eve hats or horns, heart-shaped boxes of Valentine's Day candy, American flags, or Christmas ornaments, each with an invitation attached.

Hand-printed with crayons. One of the most clever baby shower invitations I ever received was printed with crayon on an 8½" x 11" piece of construction paper. The letters were misspelled, crooked, and upside down, as if written by a small child. You can hand-print each invitation individually, or you can make up one master copy and duplicate it on a color printer.

Theme-related shapes. You can make your own theme-related invitations out of poster board. Make a pattern that relates to your party theme, such as a teddy bear, stork, pacifier, or a cowboy hat, and trace it on the poster board. Write your party invitation on one side, tie with a ribbon and mail.

Customized hospital bracelets. Make your own hospital bracelets. Cut white poster board into strips. Print the party invitation on both sides of each strip, cover with clear contact paper and form into a bracelet by stapling or taping ends together.

Plastic baby bib. Bibs can be used as invitations by writing the information across the front with marking pens. Fold and enclose in envelopes.

Birth certificates. Use parchment paper to create miniature "birth certificates." Use a calligraphy pen to fill in the blanks with the party information.

Helium balloons. Write the party invitation on each balloon before inflating with helium and tying with a long ribbon. They can be hand delivered or mailed in square boxes; when each box is opened by the recipient, the helium balloon will float to the ceiling.

Tip: If you decide to have your novelty invitations hand-delivered, why not go all out and have them delivered by someone dressed to fit the theme of your party? For example, if it's a Mother Goose shower, have the invitations delivered by someone dressed up as a nursery rhyme character, such as Humpty Dumpty or the Big Bad Wolf; if it's a Hawaiian luau, have the invitations delivered by someone dressed in a Hawaiian shirt, hat, and flowered lei.

Of course, regardless of the theme, you can always have the invitations delivered by someone dressed up as a stork.

SAMPLE INVITATIONS

Here are examples of formal and informal invitations that you can modify to suit your specific needs.

Formal

This is a sample formal invitation that can be hand-written with black ink on fine-quality white or ivory stationery, professionally engraved, laser-printed, or handwritten by a professional calligrapher.

Robert and Patricia Anderson
request the pleasure of your company
at a dinner party in honor of
Thomas and Elizabeth Daniels
and their new baby girl, Anna Marie
on June twenty-third
at seven in the evening
at two-hundred Grapevine Lane
RSVP 555-2930

Tip: You can replace the "RSVP" with "Regrets Only," so that only those who are unable to attend will need to call you.

Informal

Here are examples of informal invitations that may be handwritten, laser printed, or handmade:

Tip: If you don't have access to a computer and a printer, use the personalizer machine at any Hallmark store to compose your own invitations on the spot.

Hawaiian Luau

> ❀ *Aloha!* ❀
>
> *Grab your ukulele! Don your grass skirt!*
> *Practice your hula!*
> *Then join us for a luau baby shower*
>
> ❀
>
> **For:** *Our favorite mommy- and daddy-to-be,*
> *Cathy and Bryan*
> **When:** *Friday, July 11, at 6 p.m.*
> **Where:** *Jim and Tracy's patio/pool*
> *912 Wellingham Court*
> **Bring:** *Your swim suits and your appetites*
> **RSVP:** *555-9953 or gstone@sti.com*

Family Shower

> We're Adding to Our Family Tree
>
> ~ ❀ ~
>
> Come help us celebrate at a
> Potluck Picnic Shower
> In honor of: Kevin and Tracy and
> Baby Boy Jensen (expected to arrive on August 15)
> When: Saturday, June 20
> Time: 1 p.m.
> Where: Swan Lake Park
> Menlo Drive and S. Main
> RSVP: Paul and Ginny at 555-1779

Mother Goose Shower

Rock-a-bye baby on the treetop
When the wind blows the cradle will rock
Please come prepared to sing or recite
A rhyme or a lullaby for baby's delight

For: Our favorite mommy- and daddy-to-be,
Heather & James
When: Friday night, July 11
Time: 7 p.m.
Where: Tim and Beth's apartment
227 Arlington Place, No. 202
RSVP: 555-3301 or Galway@aol.com

Office Party

Office Memo

To: All Employees
From: Judy Harrington & Donna Martin
Date: September 1, 1998
Re: New Arrival Expected

Join us for a Baby Shower Luncheon at
Summerfield's Restaurant
over the lunch hour
Wednesday, September 16
in honor of our mommy-to-be, Sue Bennett
(Hint, hint—She's expecting a girl!)
RSVP to Judy at X337 or jhas@aol.com

Adopted Baby Celebration

> ### Come help us celebrate
> with Jim and Gail Bowen
> the arrival of their new baby boy
> Name: Kevin James
> Age: 4 months
> What: A spaghetti feed
> When: Saturday night, November 15
> Time: 6 p.m.
> Where: 2021 Winding Lane Court
> Hosted by the Randalls and the Wilsons
> RSVP: 555-9953 by November 8
> Sizes: "6 months" to "2 years"

General Baby Shower

> *You're Invited to a*
> ### Baby Shower
>
> *For:* _____
> *Date:* _____
> *Time:* _____
> *Place:* _____
> *Given by:* _____
>
> *RSVP:*_____

Chapter 8

Finding the Perfect Decorations

When we think of baby shower decorations, we usually think in terms of pale pink, blue, or yellow, but these traditional pastels have given way to bright primary colors, such as reds, blues, and greens. So, unless you have your heart set on using pastels or your theme specifically calls for one of them, keep bright primary colors in mind as you plan your decorations.

You can purchase ready-made baby shower decorations from your local party supply store, or, depending on your theme, you may be able to use something you already have around the house, such as an old cradle or bassinet that can be spray painted and decorated as a gift display, or clusters of baby bottles filled with fresh flowers that can be arranged on the serving table.

There are also simple theme-related ways to create favors, name tags, place cards, napkins rings, and centerpieces, but before we get into these details, let's begin with some of the easiest and most affordable ways to decorate for any party.

BIGGEST DECORATING BANGS FOR THE BUCK

Flowers. Whether the theme is formal or informal, flowers will create a festive spirit. You can order arrangements from your retail or supermarket florist, or you can make them yourself from any fresh or silk flowers you have available. Potted plants also work well as centerpieces, especially for a patio party or a barbecue, and you can use silk plants and ficus trees to frame your room, decorating them for the party with ribbons, tiny white Christmas lights, or tulle bows.

You'll also want to provide a corsage for the mother-to-be, a boutonniere for the father-to-be, and corsages for any expectant grandmothers in attendance. Whether you order the corsages from a professional florist or you make them yourself, you can add novelty items appropriate to the shower's theme. For example, you could add stuffed baby socks or booties, a pacifier, a rattle or a tiny teddy bear. Use diaper pins to pin the corsages and boutonniere on the honored guests. Don't forget to add a few sprigs of baby's breath to your centerpieces and corsages. After all, what could be more appropriate for a baby shower?

Note: If the meal is a sit-down dinner, be sure the centerpieces are low enough so the guests can see each other across the tables.

Tip: A floral arrangement or potted plant can double as a gift for the expectant parents or as a door prize for one of your guests.

Balloons. Helium-filled balloon bouquets can be used as table centerpieces, tied to chair-backs or napkin rings or set on the floor as "fillers" of color. Tie a few balloons to the gate or near the front door, or use them to decorate the honored guests' chairs and the gift table.

To cut down on cost, purchase your balloons in bulk from a party supply store and rent your own helium tank.

Banners. You can purchase banners from your party supply store or you can create personalized banners out of poster paper or by generating them on your computer. One of my favorite graphics programs for banners is Print Shop Deluxe.

Tip: Decorate your banners with wallpaper border that complements your theme, such as Mother Goose or Disney characters. You can run the border along the top, or you can cut out the characters and glue them to your banner.

Candles. There's nothing quite like candlelight to soften a party setting and give it an elegant, romantic ambience. Arrange floating candles, a group of votive candles, or single candles inside hurricane lamps, surrounded by fresh or silk flowers; or cluster a group of long tapered candles mounted in elegant candlesticks of various heights.

Tip: Except in the bathroom, don't use scented candles; they'll detract from the flavor of the food.

Tiny white Christmas tree lights. These tiny white lights do wonders for a setting, creating a magical ambience, especially for an evening affair. Wind a string of lights down the center of the serving tables, around silk ficus trees, or drape them over doorways or along banisters.

Crepe paper streamers. Tastefully used, crepe paper streamers are an affordable way to splash a little color around your party site.

NAME TAGS

Unless you're hosting an intimate party of close friends and family members where everyone already knows each other, it's a good idea to furnish each guest with a name tag. They can be purchased from your party supply store or you can create your own, depending on the party's theme. For example, you can cut simple shapes out of construction paper (see Appendix).

- ◆ Teddy bears for a Teddy Bear Shower.
- ◆ Trains for a Caboose Shower.
- ◆ Family trees for a Family Shower.
- ◆ Watering cans for a Country Garden Party.

And some novelty name tags are:

♦ Plastic visors with the guests' names written with permanent felt-tip markers.

♦ Purchased or homemade baby bibs with the guests' names written across the front. The guests wear these bibs throughout the party.

♦ Actual lollipops with the guests' names attached. Pin the lollipops on the guests' clothing using diaper pins.

Tips:

Don't use address labels as name tags because they'll fall off halfway through the party. If you're going to use name tags with adhesive, purchase tags designed for this purpose.

Place the name tag on the guest's right shoulder so it will be easy to see as the guests shake hands.

TABLE SETTING

There are many ways to liven up the decor by simply being creative and original in how you set the tables.

Tablecloths

If it is a formal affair, use linen tablecloths or lace cloths laid over solid color liners. Otherwise, you can use paper tablecloths or theme-related flat twin-sized sheets. Try using pink tablecloths with blue paper plates, or vice versa.

Napkins

For an informal buffet or an outdoor barbecue, you can wrap the napkins around sets of utensils, tie them with ribbons and place them in a basket. Or you can roll each napkin longways (from corner to corner) and tie it around the handles of the utensils. For a more formal affair, such as a sit-down dinner or a formal afternoon tea, you may want to fold the napkins into one of the many elegant designs that are so popular these days. Of course, napkin folding is an art of its own and the more intricate patterns aren't easy to learn, but here are three of the easier folds:

- **The fan fold.** Fold the napkin in half and, starting at one end, fold it back and forth until you have a "fan." The napkin can then be tied at the base, leaving it in the shape of a fan, tied in the center, or folded over and placed inside a long-stemmed glass.

- **The simple roll.** Fold the napkin in half and simply roll it up. Tie it in the center with gold braid or ribbon, with a silk or fresh flower attached.

- **The roll with flared top.** Fold the napkin in half and roll it up. Tie the bottom of the roll with three strips of tulle netting. Flare the top of the rolled napkin.

Novelty Napkins

Cloth Diapers. Cloth diapers, in white, colors, or prints work great for a baby shower. Fold the diaper into a triangular shape and close with a diaper pin (see Chp. 7).

Baby Bibs. Use baby bibs instead of napkins. Buy them on sale or make your own by trimming inexpensive terry cloth hand towels with grosgrain ribbon that can be purchased in bulk from a fabric store. To personalize the bibs, write each guest's name with a permanent textile marking pen or laundry marker.

Napkin Rings

Whether your party is formal or informal, it's nice to dress up your napkins with rings or ribbons. Here are a few cute napkin rings for informal baby showers:

- **Pacifiers with looped handles.** Nothing sets a table at a baby shower like pacifier napkin rings—your guests will love them!

- **Diaper pins.** Fold your napkin into the shape of a diaper and pin it closed with a diaper pin. The diaper pins can serve as place cards as well if you paint the guests' names on the pins with craft paint. Or you can use the diaper pin to secure a place card to the napkin.
- **Baby rattles with looped handles.** The same idea works with baby rattles. You can personalize the rattles by writing the guests names with a craft pen or laundry marker, in which case they will also serve as place cards.

Tableware

Formal tableware. A formal party requires glass or china plates and stemware, as well as silver or high-quality stainless utensils.

Informal tableware. An informal party allows the use of paper plates and cups and plastic utensils, but if you do decide to use paper plates, buy the best. They should not only be sturdy to prevent mishaps, but colorful, adding to your party's theme. By the way, whether you use glass or plastic stemware, you can decorate the stems with ribbons and silk flowers.

Novelty Baby Bottle Glasses

A popular novelty is to use baby bottles instead of glassware to serve the guests drinks. You can remove the nipple and insert a straw. The bottles can then be washed and given to the mom-to-be to add to her stock.

Place cards

Many of the favors listed on the following pages can also serve as place cards by simply attaching name cards to the favors and placing them at the place settings. Or you can take ordinary white place cards and dress them up in one of these easy ways:

- **Names written in silver or gold.** Write the guests' names with a silver or gold glitter pen.

- ◆ **Lace border.** Hot-glue a border of ruffled lace.
- ◆ **Bow and flowers.** Hot-glue a narrow acetate bow and tiny silk flowers.
- ◆ **Card with rosebud.** Punch a hole on each side of a standard white place card and thread a rosebud horizontally through the holes.
- ◆ **Gold or silver braid.** Hot-glue a border of gold or silver braid.

Novelty place cards

Decorated cookies. Buy or bake giant sugar cookies and write the guests' names in frosting, using a cake-decorating kit. (See Chapter 14 for Sugar Cookie recipe.)

Lollipops or candy sacks. Write the guests' names in frosting, using a cake decorating kit, across large, flat lollipops. Use the lollipops as place cards, or attach them to sacks of candy made by wrapping clear cellophane around a nut cup filled with candy and tied at the neck of the lollipop with ribbon.

Egg in egg cup or tiny basket. Hard boil one egg per guest. Decorate the eggs with Easter egg dye, writing the guests' names near the tops of the eggs. Display the eggs in soft-boiled egg cups, tiny baskets filled with Easter basket grass, or homemade egg cups made from egg cartons (cut out each section and spray gold or white).

Construction paper shapes. Create personalized place cards in a shape that relates to your theme, such as a cowboy hat, folded diaper, or miniature train caboose.

Mug or tea cup. Paint the guests' names on small mugs or tea cups using polyester craft paint. Tie the handles with narrow ribbon.

Refrigerator magnet. Use acrylic paint to write each guest's name on a refrigerator magnet cut from wood. Use a hot-glue gun to attach a 3/4" magnet to the back of each piece of wood.

Tiny teddy bears. Set a teddy bear at each place with the guest's name attached to a ribbon that is tied around the bear's neck. (Inexpensive bears are available in the crafts/fabric department at Wal-Mart stores.)

Baby bibs. Set a cloth or plastic baby bib at each place with the guest's name written across the front. Ask the guests to wear their bibs throughout the meal.

Baby's teething biscuits. Place one teething biscuit at each place with the guest's name attached to a ribbon that is tied around the middle of the biscuit.

Baby food jars full of candy. Fill clean, empty baby food jars (labels still attached) with pastel after-dinner mints. Tie ribbons around their necks and place one at each place setting.

PARTY FAVORS

Party favors are usually set at each guest's table setting or they may be placed in a theme-related container, such as an upside-down cowboy hat, or a doll-sized crib or bassinet.

You can purchase ready-made favors for your party or you can make your own. Here are a few creative, do-it-yourself ideas:

◆ **Baby bottles filled with candies.** Purchase small plastic baby bottles and fill them with candies such as jelly beans. Tie a ribbon around the top of each bottle.

◆ **Lollipops.** Place one large lollipop at each place setting. Tie a ribbon around the neck of each lollipop.

◆ **Miniature flower pots.** Fill miniature flower pots with plants or flowers and wrap them with fabric, tissue paper, or tulle netting and tie them with a ribbon.

◆ **Mug with flowers.** Purchase inexpensive, colorful mugs and fill them with flowers or a plant. Tie a bow around the handle of each mug.

◆ **Marshmallow booties.** Use toothpicks to attach three large marshmallows together in an L-shape to form each bootie. Frost each "bootie" with buttercream frosting using a cake-decorating tip. Tie a narrow satin acetate ribbon around the neck of each bootie. Set a pair of booties at each place setting.

◆ **Paper-chain necklaces.** Make a child's paper chain necklace for each guest. Place it in the center of the plate. Ask the guests to wear their necklaces during the party.

◆ **Crackers.** Crackers are novelty favors created out of crepe paper, tissue paper, and a cardboard toilet tissue tube. Wrap candies, mints, or any small novelty-type gift with tissue paper and stuff it inside the toilet tissue tube. Then wrap the tube longways with a piece of crepe paper (or giftwrapping paper) approximately 9" x 12" in size; the paper should extend past the ends of the tube about 3 inches on each end. Tie each end tightly with a colorful ribbon. Decorate the center of the crackers with colorful stickers or cut-outs that coordinate with your theme.

◆ **Mini cowboy hats.** Fill miniature cowboy hats with trail mix, wrap with tulle netting, and tie with a narrow ribbon. (You can make your own trail mix out of M&Ms, peanuts, and raisins).

◆ **"Diapered" nut cups.** Wrap nut cups with paper diapers, pinned in front with a diaper pin. Fill the cups with nuts or candy.

◆ **Rubber duckies.** Place a rubber duckie in the center of each place setting—tie a ribbon around its neck.

◆ **Helium-filled balloons.** Prepare plenty of pink and blue balloons. Tie them with long strings and let them float up to the ceiling. After they have served as room decorations, give them to the guests as they leave the party.

♦ **Miniature storks.** A miniature stork can be created with
a marshmallow body, toothpick legs, and black gumdrop
feet. Squeeze the top of the marshmallow into the shape
of its head. Add a beak formed from a doubled-over
orange toothpick. Tie a tiny white diaper to the beak.
Stand a stork in the center of each place setting.

TABLE CENTERPIECES

You can use a professional floral arrangement or a decorated
cake for your table centerpiece, or you can use one of these clever,
do-it-yourself alternatives.

Theme-Related Containers

Arrange fresh or silk flowers in a theme-related container, such
as:

♦ Spray-painted watering can or decorative bird cage for a
Country Garden Party.

♦ "Diaper" a round bowl (preferably a small fish bowl)
with a triangular-shaped piece of white flannel fabric,
pinning it closed in front with a large diaper pin. Fill the
bowl with fresh or dried flowers, or a plant. (At the end
of the party this container can double as a door prize or
as a gift from the hostess to the guest-of-honor.)

♦ Ten-gallon hat or cowboy boots for a "Little Cowboy" or
"Cowgirl" Barbecue.

Novelty Centerpieces

Depending on the theme, you can create a unique, one-of-a-kind
table centerpiece with such things as:

♦ Antique doll display for a Dolly Shower.

♦ Small toy doll buggy with *two* babies, for a Twice as
Nice shower.

- "The Three Bears" clustered together—Daddy Bear, Mommy Bear, and Baby Bear.

- Winken, Blinken, and Nod sailing across the sea (a mirror) in a wooden shoe for a Mother Goose Shower.

- An arrangement of the mother- and father-to-be's baby photos or a poster-sized enlargement of one of the mother's baby pictures, mounted on an easel.

- Large fishbowls with live goldfish for a Hawaiian Luau.

- A flock of rubber duckies floating across a pond (large round or oval mirror). Tie pink or blue ribbons around the duckies' necks.

- Inverted colander filled with lollipops stuck in the holes. Tie each lollipop with a pink or blue ribbon. Use heart-shaped lollipops for a Valentine's Day baby shower.

- Miniature clothesline and clothespins holding baby bibs, miniature diapers, baby clothes or doll clothes.

- An electric train running around a track.

- A small silk ficus tree or artificial Christmas tree hung with small snapshots of family members, plus a tiny basket holding a miniature baby suspended from one of the branches. The basket can be inscribed with the baby's name if one has already been chosen.

- A man's boot with a cardboard roof, a doll mother, and many tiny plastic babies crawling in, over, and around the shoe, simulating the "Woman Who Lived in a Shoe" (for a nursery rhyme theme).

- A fake spider suspended from the ceiling by fishing line, hovering over the head of "Miss Muffet" (for a Mother Goose theme).

- "Little Boy Blue" asleep on a pile of hay (for a Nursery Rhyme theme).

- If it's Christmas time, use a miniature sleigh as the centerpiece with a bundled-up baby doll sitting inside. If you have a Santa and reindeer to add to the display, all the better.

- If it's Easter time, make a giant egg by wrapping a fish bowl with heavy white paper cut into a zig-zag at the top. Fill the egg with Easter basket grass and a baby peeking out over the top. Place colored Easter eggs around the baby.

- If it's around Valentine's day, sit a baby doll on a heart-shaped pink cushion.

- Make a sugar plum tree by spray-painting a tree branch white, inserting it into a block of modeling clay for stability, and decorating it with gum drops, candy kisses, and tiny satin ribbons. Sprinkle the ground beneath the tree with brown sugar and more gum drops that have "dropped" from the tree. Surround the tree with a fence made out of tiny peppermint sticks inserted into marshmallow bases.

NOVELTY DECORATIONS

Children's art work. Enlist the help of a kindergarten teacher friend or ask any small children you may know to create colorful art-work that can be hung around the room as party decorations. Furnish construction paper in colors that complement your party theme and ask the children to draw pictures of the new mommy with her baby, of the new daddy at the hospital, or the new family all together back home (including the family pets). These colorful drawings will not only decorate your party site, but will serve as conversation pieces during the party. Then, of course, they can be given to the expectant parents as mementos of the party.

Tip: Instead of single sheets of construction paper, have the children create a mural on a continuous roll of white shelf paper. This mural can eventually be used as a wall decoration for baby's nursery.

Giant peppermint sticks. Giant peppermint sticks are perfect for a Sugar Plum Tree theme. Cover tall cardboard cylinders by winding with strips of pink and white crepe paper. Use the peppermint sticks to frame your front door, your serving table, or the gift display area.

Six-foot stork. Borrow or rent a free-standing stork from a florist, party supply store, or your local baby store.

Neon sign. Rent a neon sign for your window that says "It's a Boy," "Congratulations," etc. (Look under "Signs" or "Neon Signs" in your Yellow Pages. The signs can usually be rented by the day or week.)

Suspended baby items. Use fishing line to suspend small baby-related items from the ceiling, such as rattles, pacifiers, rubber duckies, etc. Or you can use pink and blue poster board to create cardboard shapes such as storks, rocking horses, baby bottles, booties, bibs, teddy bears, folded diapers, or babies.

Miniature baby nursery. Use toy nursery furniture to set up a miniature baby nursery in the corner of the room, complete with a "baby," a child-sized rocking chair, a little crib, etc. Or create a baby nursery centerpiece for your serving table by assembling pieces of doll house furniture.

Tip: One hostess I interviewed said she used this idea as a guessing game for the mommy-to-be. She had a complete nursery set up with one important piece of furniture missing. She asked the guest of honor to look carefully at the display to see what was missing. The missing item turned out to be a joint shower gift from all the guests.

Clothesline strung with diapers. String a clothesline across the room or behind the serving table. Use clothespins to attach diapers, baby rattles, stuffed animals, etc.

Tip: This is also a quick and easy decoration for an office party.

Note: See Chapter 10 for gift display ideas.

Chapter 9

Choosing Games and Entertainment

Boring baby shower games are a thing of the past; today's parties can be *much* more fun.

This chapter is filled with the most popular baby shower games and activities. As you consider the various options, keep several things in mind: the formality of your party, the theme of your party, and the ages of your guests. The idea is to choose games and activities that will come as close as possible to pleasing everyone. Obviously, if your guests already know each other, you won't need icebreaker activities and if everyone seems to be chatting away and enjoying each other's company, you may decide to dispense with games altogether.

You should also keep the time factor in mind. If you're planning a two-hour shower, you'll probably want to allow no more than 30 to

40 minutes of that time for games. That will leave about an hour and a half for the refreshments and the opening of the gifts.

GET-ACQUAINTED GAMES

Get-acquainted activities are great icebreakers, especially when there is a mixed group of guests, perhaps consisting of family members and the expectant parents' co-workers and friends.

Who Am I?

Preparation:

- ◆ 3 x 5 cards; one per guest.
- ◆ Safety pins; one per guest.
- ◆ Write the name of a Mother Goose or Disney character on each card.

This is a great get-acquainted game because it forces the guests to talk to each other. Pin one of these cards to each player's back. Each person can see the names on the backs of the other guests, but can't, of course, see her own. The idea of the game is for a player to determine which children's character is pinned on her back by asking questions.

As the game begins, each player is allowed to ask three questions per round. Questions must be answered only with a yes or no. For example, "Was I a character in a Disney movie?"

The first player to guess the character on her back wins a prize. By the way, be sure to have extra prizes on hand in case of a tie.

Diaper Pin Game

Preparation:

- ◆ One diaper pin per guest.

Purchase a supply of diaper pins. Pin one diaper pin on each guest's clothing and let the game begin. Set a timer for 20 minutes.

During that 20-minute period no one is allowed to say the word *no*. So, the idea of the game is to ask the guests questions about themselves, baiting them to answer with a *no*. Any guest who does must relinquish her diaper pin to the person who tricked her into saying the forbidden word. When the timer dings, the guest with the most diaper pins wins.

Baby Identification Game

Preparation:

- ♦ One baby picture from each guest.
- ♦ Paper and pencils for each guest.
- ♦ A bulletin board or cork board.
- ♦ Stick pins or thumb tacks.

When you send out the party invitations, request a baby picture from each person. After all the guests have arrived at the party and supplied you with their baby photos, assign each photo a number and pin it on the bulletin board. The guests are given paper and pencils and 10 minutes to guess the identity of each photo. The person who correctly identifies the most baby photos wins.

BABY SHOWER FAVORITES

Mother Goose Charades

Preparation:

- ♦ Copy the first lines of the nursery rhymes given on pages 78 and 79 onto individual pieces of paper.
- ♦ Two pens.
- ♦ Two baskets.
- ♦ A timer.
- ♦ For "Pictionary" version: One easel with large pad of paper and a box of crayons.

Charades is truly an all-American favorite. Divide the guests into two teams—evenly mixed men and women or the men against the women, older generation against younger generation, etc. Give each team a basket that contains five or six pieces of paper containing the first lines of nursery rhymes.

Team members must take turns drawing one of these pieces of paper from the basket and are given two or three minutes to silently act out the nursery rhyme, using hands, body, and facial expressions to communicate. If the timer dings before the team has guessed the nursery rhyme, the opposing team gets five points. If the team guesses it before the timer dings, they get 10 points. After each side has had five or six turns, the team with the most points wins. In the case of a tie, play one more round.

Another version of this game is to draw the clues, instead of act them out, resulting in a game similar to "Pictionary."

Note: Not everyone is comfortable "acting out" in front of a group, so it's a good idea to have less turns per side than there are team members. This will allow team members to decline graciously without feeling pressured.

Here are the first lines of nursery rhymes:

♦ Little Jack Horner sat in a corner eating a Christmas pie.

♦ Wee Willie Winkie runs through the town, upstairs and downstairs in his nightgown.

♦ There was a little girl and she had a little curl right in the middle of her forehead.

♦ Jack and Jill went up a hill to fetch a pail of water.

♦ Humpty Dumpty sat on a wall, Humpty Dumpty had a great fall.

♦ Georgie Porgie, pudding and pie, kissed the girls and made them cry.

♦ Tom, Tom, the piper's son stole a pig and away he run.

♦ Mary, Mary, quite contrary, how does your garden grow?

- Little Boy Blue, come blow your horn.
- Jack be nimble, Jack be quick, Jack jump over the candle-stick.
- Mary had a little lamb, its fleece was white as snow.
- There was a crooked man and he went a crooked mile.
- Hey diddle diddle, the cat and the fiddle, the cow jumped over the moon.
- There was an old woman who lived in a shoe.
- Old King Cole was a merry old soul and a merry old soul was he.
- Little Bo-Peep has lost her sheep and can't tell where to find them.
- Little Miss Muffet sat on a tuffet, eating her curds and whey.

Baby Bonnet Contest

Preparation:

- Large supply of crepe paper.
- Large supply of tissue paper and paper napkins.
- One paper doily per guest.
- Ribbons, lace, and scraps of fabric.
- Several pair of scissors.
- Scotch tape.
- Safety pins.
- Stapler (with plenty of extra staples).

Here is a silly, but fun, contest. Ask the guests to fashion baby bonnets for *themselves* out of the supplies you have furnished. Tell them there will be prizes for "Most Creative," "Cutest," "Silliest," etc. Ask the guests to wear their baby bonnets for the remainder of the party.

Tip: This is a lot of fun at a co-ed party when the men join in.

The Parents' Game

Preparation:

- ♦ 20 sheets of 8½" x 11" paper.
- ♦ Four felt tip pens.

This game is played the same way as the Newlywed Game, except the contestants are parents. Four couples are chosen to compete. The men leave the room and the women are asked questions, and their answers are recorded on sheets of paper.

The men come back into the room and are asked the same questions. The object is for the men to respond with the same answers as their partners. Then, the game is reversed and the women leave the room as the men are asked questions, and so forth. The couple with the most matching answers wins.

Here are some typical questions:

- ♦ What will your spouse say was the worst thing about the delivery?
- ♦ Who does the baby look like?
- ♦ How many times has Daddy changed a dirty diaper?
- ♦ How many times has Daddy gotten up with the baby in the middle of the night?

The Observation Game

Preparation:

- ♦ One large tray.
- ♦ 20 or 30 small baby-related items.
- ♦ One sheet of paper and pencil per guest.

On a tray, arrange baby-related items, such as a rattle, a baby spoon, a diaper pin, and so forth. Then ask someone, such as the expectant mother's sister, to walk slowly around the room, displaying the tray for all the guests to see.

As soon as the tray is taken out of the room, the guests will be asked to write down as many items as they can remember. The guest who remembers the most items receives a prize.

A fun variation of this game is to ask them to write down as many things as they can remember about the person carrying the tray (color of hair and eyes; what she was wearing, etc.)!

The guests will moan and cry "foul," of course, but they'll finally settle down and start recording things they remember. The guest who has recorded the most accurate description wins a prize.

Baby Diapering Contest

Preparation:

- One large baby doll or teddy bear.
- One cloth diaper.
- Two diaper pins.
- One pair of mittens (for the women only).
- Stopwatch (or a watch with a second hand).

The guests take turns diapering the doll or bear. The women are required to wear mittens; the men are not. The guest is disqualified if the diaper falls off when the doll or bear is held up and wiggled in the air. The person with the fastest time wins.

Another variation of this game is to have the contestant wear a blindfold while diapering the doll or bear.

Mystery Baby Food Game

Preparation:

- 10 jars of baby food.
- Paper and pencil for each guest.
- One small plastic spoon per guest.

Cover the labels on 10 jars of baby food, such as pears, squash, sweet potatoes, bananas, etc. Number them from 1 to 10. Give each guest paper, a pencil, and a small plastic spoon. Pass the jars around the room, one at a time. The guests must identify the food by sight, smell, and taste. (Each guest is instructed to dip the tip of the spoon into the food.) The guest with the most correct answers wins.

Tip: If you really want to make this game challenging, add a few of the new "gourmet" baby food mixtures, such as apples and chicken, pear and wild blueberry, or chicken and rice.

Diaper Game

Preparation:

♦ Nine cloth diapers.

♦ A pointer (a yardstick will do).

Place nine cloth diapers on the floor in this exact order:

□	□	□
1	2	3
□	□	□
4	5	6
□	□	□
7	8	9

The idea of this game is to have your guests figure out which diaper is "it" by the way you point to the diapers and ask, "Is this one 'it'?" (Use a yardstick as a pointer).

There are usually one or two guests who are familiar with this game and know immediately which diaper is "it" by watching for the secret clue, which is revealed by *where* you touch the *first* diaper you point to. Picture in your mind that the first diaper you touch is a map of all nine diapers. If you've decided that diaper number 3 is to be *it* for the first round of the game, you should point to the upper right hand corner of the first diaper you touch. (It doesn't matter which diaper you touch first, it can even be the diaper that is *it*.) Once you've given the clue with the first touch, you continue the game by touching *any* spot on *any* of the nine diapers and continue asking, "Is this one *it*?"

If a player doesn't know the game, she'll try to figure it out by listening for the inflection in your voice, by whether you rub your chin or touch your eye as you point to a diaper, or whether you change the wording of your question a little when you finally point to *it*.

The fun for those "in the know," of course, is that they're aware of the secret clue and get a charge out of watching everyone else as they struggle along, and the fun for the strugglers is in the challenge of figuring it out.

After several rounds where only one or two guests have caught on each time, you'll need to "give it away" by exaggerating your first point.

This game can take from 30 minutes to an hour, depending on how much the guests seem to be enjoying the challenge.

Nursery Rhyme Clap-a-Thon

Preparation:

♦ None.

Divide the guests into two teams. Each team decides which nursery rhymes they want the opposing team to "clap out" in rhythm. Each team claps out the rhythms of the nursery rhymes picked by the other team. The idea, of course, is to choose nursery rhymes that are difficult to clap out. The team that can identify the most nursery rhymes wins.

Tip: This game gets easier as it goes along and the ear becomes accustomed to listening for the rhythm of the words. Clap out "Hickory, Dickory, Dock" and you'll see what I mean.

"Hickory, dickory, dock,
The mouse ran up the clock.
The clock struck one,
The mouse ran down.
Hickory, dickory, dock."

Potty Toss

Preparation:

♦ One child's potty (the cuter, the better).

♦ 10 large diaper pins.

Place a child's potty on the floor, about 10 feet away from the contestant. The contestant is given 10 diaper pins to toss into the potty, one at a time. The guest with the most "ringers" wins. In case of a tie, have a play-off.

Name That Tune

Preparation:

♦ Several kazoos.

♦ A children's songbook (available at your local library), if you're unfamiliar with children's songs.

This is similar to the "Clap-a-Thon," except that the team members play a children's song on a kazoo. The object is to correctly identify the name of the tune. Here are a few typical children's songs that are easy to identify by the melody:

♦ "Hey, Diddle Diddle"

♦ "Baa, Baa, Black Sheep"

♦ "The Farmer in the Dell"

♦ "Hot Cross Buns"

♦ "London Bridge Is Falling Down"

- "Mary Had a Little Lamb"
- "Do You Know the Muffin Man?"
- "The Mulberry Bush"
- "Old Mac Donald Had a Farm"
- "Pease Porridge Hot"
- "Pop Goes the Weasel"
- "Rock-a-Bye Baby"
- "Three Blind Mice"
- "Twinkle, Twinkle, Little Star"

Baby Bottle Race

Preparation:

- One baby bottle filled with juice per contestant.

This is a hilarious game for a co-ed party. Volunteer the men to be contestants in this race. The first man to empty his bottle of juice wins. The humor, of course, is that the men are required to suck their bottles dry through ordinary baby bottle nipples.

Tip: No cheating allowed! Clever contestants have been known to "accidentally" bite the ends off the nipples!

Scavenger Hunt

Preparation:

- Photocopy the list of items given below—one copy per guest.
- One pen or pencil per guest.
- A timer.

This hunt takes place inside the women's purses. Set the timer for four minutes and see how many of these items each woman can find in her handbag. The guest with the most points wins.

....

20 points per item:

$100 bill	_____	Cotton swabs	_____
Silver dollar	_____	Alarm clock	_____
Dental floss	_____	Pair of gloves	_____
Toothbrush	_____	Pocket knife	_____
Dictionary	_____	Photo of mother	_____
Smelling salts	_____	Candy bar	_____
Magnifying glass	_____	Cigar	_____
Nail polish		Fresh fruit	_____
remover	_____	Cellular phone	_____

10 points per item:

Postage stamps	_____	Pain reliever	_____
Scissors	_____	Rubber band	_____
Pencil with an		Tweezers	_____
eraser	_____	Nail clippers	_____
Cloth hanky	_____	Breath mints	_____
Address book	_____	Calculator	_____
Eyelash curler	_____	Notebook	_____
Mascara	_____	Photos of pets	_____
Face powder	_____	Shopping list	_____

5 points per item:

Lipstick/lip balm	_____	Eyeglasses	_____
Hair comb	_____	Credit card	_____
Hand lotion	_____	Family photos	_____
Regular mirror	_____	Chewing gum	_____
Tissue	_____	Pen	_____
Sunglasses	_____		

Total _____

WORD GAMES

Nursery Rhyme Quiz

Preparation:

- ◆ Photocopy one copy of the quiz per guest.
- ◆ Pens or pencils.
- ◆ Timer.

Fill in the next line of each nursery rhyme:

1. Wee Willie Winkie runs through the town,

   _____

2. Bye, baby bunting, Daddy's gone a-hunting,

   _____

3. There was an old woman who lived in a shoe,

   _____

4. Old Mother Hubbard went to the cupboard,

   _____

5. Pease-porridge hot, pease-porridge cold,

   _____

6. Bobby Shafto's gone to sea, silver buckles on his knee,

   _____

7. Diddle, diddle, dumpling, my son John,

   _____

8. Sing a song of sixpence, a pocket full of rye,

   _____

Answers:

1. Upstairs and downstairs, in his nightgown.
2. Gone to get a rabbit skin to wrap a baby bunting in.
3. She had so many children she didn't know what to do.
4. To get her poor dog a bone.
5. Pease-porridge in the pot nine days old.
6. He'll come back and marry me, Bonny Bobby Shafto!
7. Went to bed with his trousers on.
8. Four and twenty blackbirds baked in a pie.

The Baby Name Game

Preparation:

♦ Photocopy the list below—one per guest.
♦ One pen or pencil per guest.
♦ A timer.

Set the timer for 10 minutes. The guest who matches the most names with their correct meanings wins a prize.

1.	Graceful	_____	Erin
2.	Gift of the Lord	_____	Trevor
3.	Honey Bee	_____	Darren
4.	Pretty	_____	Casey
5.	Peace	_____	Matthew
6.	Prudent	_____	Linda
7.	Brave	_____	Ann
8.	Grounds Keeper	_____	Jason
9.	Great	_____	Garth
10.	Healer	_____	Melissa

Answers:

1. Ann: Graceful
2. Matthew: Gift of the Lord
3. Melissa: Honey Bee
4. Linda: Pretty
5. Erin: Peace
6. Trevor: Prudent
7. Casey: Brave
8. Garth: Grounds Keeper
9. Darren: Great
10. Jason: Healer

Baby Word Scramble

Preparation:

♦ Photocopy the list below—one per guest.

♦ One pen or pencil per guest.

♦ A timer.

Here is a list of words for your guests to unscramble. Make as many copies as you need. They all have to do with babies. See who can unscramble the most words in three minutes.

1. YBBA TLOBET _____
2. SARIPED _____
3. IRCB _____
4. TLYEATE _____
5. LRDAEC _____
6. RLUMFAO _____
7. IGRNKCO HRCIA _____
8. KLEBTNA _____
9. TELTAR _____
10. CRIPEIAF _____

Answers:

1. baby bottle
2. diapers
3. crib
4. layette
5. cradle

6. formula
7. rocking chair
8. blanket
9. rattle
10. pacifier

The Word Race Game

Preparation:

♦ One sheet of lined paper per guest.

♦ One pen or pencil per guest.

♦ A timer.

See who can make the most words from any of the following words:

1. Diaper pins.
2. Jennifer/Michael (use the couple's first names).
3. Georgetown Hospital (use the name of the hospital where the baby will be born).
5. Baby formula.
6. Motherhood.

Set a timer for 10 minutes. The guest with the most words wins.

ENTERTAINING ACTIVITIES

Packing Baby's Trunk

Preparation:

♦ Compose an opening sentence.

The object of this game is for each guest to "add to baby's trunk." For example, you might say, "I'm packing baby's trunk with a dozen diapers." The next person might say, "I'm packing baby's trunk with a dozen diapers and a pair of baby booties." The third person may say, "I'm packing baby's trunk with a dozen diapers, a pair of baby booties, and a pacifier," and so forth.

The hostess usually begins the game and if there is more than a moment's hesitation before the next person begins to speak, or that person can't remember the list of things being packed for baby's trunk, that person is "out." The story continues around the circle, until only a few people are left. At that point the game picks up speed until there is only one person remaining, who is declared the winner.

Diaper Decorating Contest

Preparation:

♦ One diaper per guest.

♦ Embroidery hoops.

♦ Embroidery needles and thread.

♦ Liquid embroidery pens (available at crafts stores).

Provide each guest with one plain white cloth diaper and an embroidery hoop, liquid embroidery pens, or embroidery needles and thread. Ask the guests to decorate the seats of the diapers with something creative, such as a heart, flower, or an embroidered message. Pass the diapers around for everyone to see and give a prize for the most creative design. The diapers are then given as a gift to the guest of honor.

Guess Baby's Birthday

Preparation:

♦ Photocopy the form on the next page—enough for three per guest, just in case.

♦ Several pens and pencils.

♦ One large piggy bank.

♦ One basket or bowl.

Duplicate the form below and let everyone enter as many times as they want. Of course, each entry will cost a designated amount—usually 50 cents to $5. All the money is stuffed into a piggy bank for the baby. The guesses are placed in a basket or bowl until the baby is born.

The winner is awarded a prize, such as dinner for two at a nice restaurant, theater tickets, or a gift certificate at a local department store.

Guess Baby's Birthday

Date of Birth: _____

Time of Birth: _____

Name _____

Address _____

Telephone _____

Baby's Keepsake Quilt

Preparation:

- One solid color crib quilt.
- Embroidery hoops.
- Embroidery thread and needles.
- No. 2 pencil.
- Liquid embroidery pens (available at your local crafts store).

This is a similar idea to the Diaper Decorating Contest, except that each guest autographs the quilt, which is intended to be kept as a keepsake. Ask the guests to sign using a No. 2 pencil or a liquid embroidery pen. The penciled autographs can be embroidered with thread at a later date.

Tip: Be sure to use an embroidery hoop to stretch the fabric tight as each person signs the quilt.

Baby's Time Capsule

Have you ever built a time capsule? It's a lot of fun. The idea is to place memorabilia relevant to baby's birth year into a large decorated coffee can, cookie tin, or Tupperware bowl.

Personalize this time capsule with items you think are important in today's world, such as a newspaper article about extreme sports or the Beanie Baby rage. Or how about placing an actual Beanie Baby in the capsule? Other possibilities are magazine advertisements for this year's most popular new products, music or computer CDs, information about your town, and a Polaroid photo of everyone at the baby shower, along with written messages to the baby from everyone attending.

You'll need to add this request to your invitation so that your guests will come prepared to contribute to this fun project.

The time capsule can be opened by the child when he or she graduates from high school, gets married, etc.

Background Music

Play a tape or CD of lullabies or nursery songs softly in the background during the party.

Chapter 10

Baby Shower Gifts and Prizes

Once you've mailed out your invitations, you'll be inundated with telephone calls asking for gift ideas. If the expectant parents have established a gift registry at a baby store or department store, pass that information along. If not, here are a few gift suggestions. By the way, it's always a good idea to ask your guest(s) of honor which items they need the most and which, if any, they have already received. That way there won't be a duplication of gifts.

GIFTS FOR BABY

Basic Necessities

- Crib blankets/quilt.
- Sleepers.
- Baby towels and washcloths.
- Diapers.
- Undershirts.
- Bibs.
- Booties.
- Socks.
- Mittens.

- Plastic pants.
- Baby bottles.
- Receiving blankets.
- Nursery jar set.
- Crib sheets.
- Sweater and cap set.
- Crib bumpers.
- Diaper pail.
- Diaper pins.
- Diaper bag.
- Infant seat.
- Tipper cup.
- Waterproof lap pads.
- Baby powder, shampoo, oil, soap.
- Outfits, in newborn and infant sizes.

Note: The parents of an older adopted child may appreciate larger-sized clothes and more advanced toys, such as a tricycle, doll house, electric train, and so forth.

Tip: Some hostesses request that each guest bring a small box of disposable diapers (any size) in addition to their main gift.

Would Be Nice to Have

- Tights.
- Insulated baby bottle carrier.
- Baby hangers.
- Crib toys.
- Brush and comb set.
- Crib pillow and pillowcases.
- Baby record book.
- Parenting books/magazines.
- Growth chart.
- Feeding spoon.
- Baby bathtub.
- Baby thermometer.
- Outfits, ranging from size 12 months to 2T.*
- Nursery decorations, such as a mobile or switch plate covers.
- Bath thermometer.
- Stuffed animals.
- Gift certificate for a professional baby portrait.
- Rattles and teething rings.
- Baby scissors.
- Shoes.
- Baby food grinder.

- Potty chair.
- Musical toys.
- Quilts.
- Plate/cup set.
- Baby scale.
- Crocheted shawl.
- Picture frames.
- Snow suit.
- Jogging suit.
- Safety gate.
- Music box.
- Portable crib.
- Booster chair.
- Baby scale.
- Dirty clothes basket.
- Waterproof mattress covers.
- Books.
- Diaper stacker.
- Night light.
- Picture album.
- Bottle warmer.
- Tub toys.
- Piggy bank.**

*Note: Many mothers I interviewed said they wished they had received larger-sized clothing because their babies outgrew the newborn-size outfits within two months.

**In some parts of the country it is a custom for the guests to stuff bills and coins into a large piggy bank as a "head start" for the baby's savings account.

More Expensive Gifts

- Crib.
- Rocking chair.
- Car seat.
- Baby swing.
- Baby walker/jumper.
- Bassinet.
- Instant thermometer (temperature taken in baby's ear).
- Cradle.
- Dressing table.
- Child's rocker.
- One year's diaper service.
- Sterling silver frame, spoon, bank, rattle, place setting, or cup.
- Intercom nursery monitor.
- Stroller.
- 14k gold locket, bracelet, or ring.

- Playpen.
- High chair.
- Toy chest.
- Christening gown.

- Starter savings account or savings bond.

Tip: If your goal is to have all the guests contribute to the purchase of one large item, such as a crib, make this clear on the invitations. You could say, "We would appreciate your contribution toward the purchase of one group gift: a much-needed crib for the nursery."

GIFTS FOR MOMMY

Hospital Basket

- Bath powder.
- Hand lotion.
- Book/magazines.
- Favorite candy bars.
- Makeup kit.
- Manicure kit.
- Hand mirror/comb.

- Hair ribbons/clips.
- Perfume or cologne.
- Pen/pencil set.
- Portable writing table.
- Stationery/thank-you notes.
- Book of postage stamps.

Breakfast-in-Bed Basket

- Breakfast tray.
- Elegant place setting of china.
- Fine linen napkin.
- China tea cup or coffee cup.

- Teapot or individual coffee carafe.
- Gourmet coffee and teas.
- Imported tea biscuits, tarts, etc.
- Box of candy.

Other Gift Ideas

- Lacy, feminine nightie.
- Satin robe.

- Satin slippers.
- Bed jacket.

- Relaxing CD or cassette tape.
- Gift certificate for a "Day at the Spa."
- Bubble bath or bath salts.
- Cosmetic case.

- Humorous coffee mug, T-shirt, or sweatshirt.
- Charm bracelet with a charm that represents the new baby.

GIFTS FOR DADDY

Hospital Survival Kit

- Candy bars.
- Book of crossword puzzles/pencil.
- Fiction or nonfiction book.
- Snacks, including granola bars.
- Cue cards for labor coaching.
- Party Gorp (see recipe in Chapter 11).
- Canned juices.
- Pain reliever.

- Sack of his favorite homemade cookies.
- Pack of chewing gum.
- List of names/telephone numbers of everyone to be called when baby is born
- Disposable indoor camera.
- Deck of cards for playing Solitaire.
- Magazines such as *Sports Illustrated*, etc.

"Bachelor" Survival Kit

- Instructions for the automatic coffee maker or a jar of instant coffee.
- Instructions on how to use the dishwasher and washer and dryer.
- Pet-feeding instructions.
- A loaf of bread and jars of peanut butter and jelly.
- More pain reliever.

- If there are other children in the family, a list of the basics (bedtimes, school times, schedules for practices, carpool info, etc.).
- Important telephone numbers, such as the hospital, the doctor, his mother-in-law, etc.
- TV dinners.
- Canned spaghetti, chili, etc.
- Snack foods, such as pretzels, nuts, and crackers and cheese.
- Fast-food gift certificates.
- Gift certificate for pizza delivery.
- Six-pack of his favorite beverage.

Humorous Gift Basket

- Large pacifier for him.
- Nodoz.
- Plastic disposable gloves, surgical mask, and nose plugs (to wear when changing diapers).
- His own personal baby bottle (purchase a huge animal-feeding bottle from a veterinarian).
- Alarm clock for the 2 a.m. feeding.
- Humorous coffee mug, T-shirt, or sweatshirt.
- Package of condoms.

Other Essentials

- Box of cigars.
- Blank video tape (for taping the new baby).
- Cassette recorder/tapes.
- Picture frame for his office.
- Autographed baseball, bat, football, etc., for the baby.
- Brag book (for baby pictures).

GIFTS FOR MOMMY AND DADDY

Gift Certificates

- Home-cooked meal brought to their door.
- One home-baked pie or cake per week for four weeks (or per month for a year).
- Pizza, KFC, or other home delivery.
- Restaurant meals.
- Free car wash.
- Free house cleaning, laundry, or yard service.
- Three free hours of running errands.
- One free month of chauffeuring duties (for any older children who need rides to/from school, soccer practice, etc.).
- Parenting advice (only when solicited).
- "First Night on the Town"—a group gift that includes several gift certificates:
  - ⇨ One free evening of baby-sitting.
  - ⇨ Corsage and boutonniere from a local florist.
  - ⇨ Dinner for two at a fine restaurant.
  - ⇨ Movie, concert, or theater tickets.
- Several movies on video tape, or a membership in a movie rental club.
- Romantic gift basket filled with champagne, cheeses, imported crackers, etc.
- Camcorder.
- Camera.
- Tape recorder.
- Film developing.

GIFTS FOR GRANDPARENTS

- Supply of disposable diapers.
- Safety railing or bed-top "napper" to make any bed safe for the baby.
- Stuffed animals.
- Receiving blankets.
- Waterproof lap pads.
- Tub toys.
- Basket filled with the basics: baby oil, baby lotion, powder, etc.
- Rattles.
- Pacifiers.
- Teething ring.
- Bibs.
- Infant feeding spoon.
- Bottles/nipples/formula.
- Safety gate.
- Crib.
- Play pen.
- High chair.
- Camcorder.
- Camera.
- Tape recorder.

GIFT DISPLAY

Although gifts can be set on a table in the corner of the room, it's much nicer to display them in a special way, creating a focal point as the guests arrive. Think about your theme and you'll come up with ideas. Here are a few examples:

- A decorated plastic or wicker laundry basket.
- A toy chest to hold the gifts (the toy chest may double as a hostess gift).
- Place the gifts under a silk ficus "sugar plum tree" decorated with lollipops, candy kisses, and gum drops.
- A decorated cradle or bassinet that can be used to hold the gifts, or you can place a doll baby inside the cradle or bassinet along with a few stuffed animals, and place the gifts on the floor beneath.
- A decorated rocking chair.
- A decorated play pen.

- A child's red wagon, decorated for the occasion.
- A corner enclosed with sections of picket fencing or wire fencing that has been spray-painted in a color to match the party's theme.
- Roll the gifts into the room on a decorated hand truck or freight dolly.
- Roll the gifts into the room in a decorated wheelbarrow.
- Hide the gifts around the house until it's time to open them. Give the mother-to-be a list of clues to follow that will lead her to the gifts. She can ask for help from the other guests if she would like. You can make up your own rhyming clues, but here are a few ideas to get you started:

> "The sugar and spice hold something nice."

> "Left, right, left, right,
> by the switch that turns on the lights."

> "A gift so tiny and small,
> it hides by the pictures on the wall."

> "On hands and knees (if you are able),
> you'll find a surprise under a table."

> "It's staring you in the face,
> try looking near the fireplace."

> "Something calls that cannot talk,
> look behind the grandfather clock."

> "A gift beautiful and new,
> hides in the closet behind the shoes."

> "A tisket, a tasket,
> look inside the basket."

> "You ought to look
> on the shelf that holds a book."

"Jack and Jill went up the hill
to hide their gift on the window sill."

"You might want to try the bathroom
just take a look behind the broom."

"Hiding near the top of the stairs,
take a peek behind the Teddy bears."

A variation of this gift hunt is to have the honored guest open small, relatively inexpensive gifts in the normal way, followed by a "Baby Treasure Hunt" where she must follow clues that lead her to one large joint gift from all the guests. Her first clue can be enclosed in the last gift-wrapped box she opens. Use the clues suggested above, except that instead of each clue leading to a gift, each clue leads to *another* clue until the large gift is finally found.

OPENING OF THE GIFTS

The gifts are usually presented to the honored guest(s) near the end of the party. One of your helpers should sit next to the guest of honor as she opens gifts to be sure the cards are kept with the gifts and to make a list of who gave what. This list is given to the mother or father-to-be after all the gifts have been opened so they can keep track of who gave them each of the gifts.

As gifts are opened they are usually passed around the room for all the guests to admire.

All the ribbons and bows from the gifts can be used to make a colorful bouquet, which will be given to the mother-to-be at the end of the party to use as a decoration in the baby's nursery. Another helper can attach the ribbons and bows to a sturdy plate to make the bouquet.

Tip: Have your guest of honor sit in a specially decorated chair as she opens her gifts.

DOOR PRIZE GIMMICKS

Guests love the idea of door prizes. These may be something you purchase and wrap ahead of time or part of your decorations, such as a table centerpiece, potted plant, or floral arrangement. Here are a few popular ways to determine who wins a door prize:

- Number the backs of the name tags and place corresponding numbers on pieces of paper that are folded up and placed in a basket. Near the end of the party, ask the guest of honor to draw a piece of paper out of the basket. The winning number receives the prize.

- Insert three wads of paper (with pre-determined numbers) inside three balloons *before* they are blown up with helium gas. Arrange the balloons in a bouquet as part of the decorations. Then, near the end of the party, ask one of the expectant parents to select one of the balloons and burst it by sitting on it (no hands allowed!) The wad of paper is then unfolded and the number read. The person with the corresponding number on the back of her name tag wins a door prize. Repeat this same procedure for the second and third balloons.

- If the party is a sit-down dinner, place a baby-related sticker under the seats of two or three of the dining room chairs. After dessert has been served, ask the guests to look under their chairs to see who has the stickers. Those who do, win prizes.

- Let the guests guess how many jelly beans or candy hearts there are in a clear glass baby bottle. The guest who comes closest to the correct answer wins the bottle full of goodies.

SUGGESTED GAME AND DOOR PRIZES

Women

- Bath powder.
- Cologne.
- Bag of potpourri.
- Decorated candle.
- Bubble bath or bath salts.
- Drawer sachets.

- Bracelet.
- Gift basket containing homemade dessert breads, jams and jellies, or bath accessories.
- Party centerpiece, floral arrangement, or decoration.
- Sunshade for her car.
- Picture frame.
- Compact.

Men

- Humorous tie.
- Four-pack of cigars.
- Gift certificate for a car wash.
- Gift certificate from a sporting goods store.
- Pen and pencil set.
- Swiss army knife.
- Desk accessories.
- Money clip.
- Travel kit.
- Sunshade for his car.
- Sports trivia book.

Co-ed

- Gift certificate to a restaurant.
- Two movie passes.
- Bucket of gourmet popcorn.
- Bottle of wine or champagne.
- Two coffee mugs and a pound of coffee beans.
- Basket of gourmet cheeses/crackers.
- Box of candy.
- Gift certificate for pizza delivery.
- Party centerpiece, floral arrangement, or decoration.

Part III

Preparing the Spread

The type of food you serve will depend on the time and theme of your party and your budget. As I've already mentioned, baby showers are no longer predictable affairs, with traditional coffee and dessert, or tea and sandwiches. In fact, there are really no rules at all—so plan any type of fare that seems comfortable for you and suitable for your theme and time of day.

In the chapters that follow you will find several popular recipes for party snacks, meals, drinks, and desserts. If your party will be a formal affair, you may want to consider an Alice in Wonderland tea party, an exquisite champagne breakfast, or an elegant sit-down dinner. Or if you're planning an informal party, there is everything from snacks and appetizers, to luncheon buffets, to clever desserts and party drinks, including the latest in trendy new "smoothies" and specialty coffees.

Have fun as you plan your menu and remember, don't plan more than you can handle. After all, you want to have fun at the party, too!

Chapter 11

Party Snacks and Appetizers

Snacks and appetizers can be given an attractive presentation by serving on large trays that have been layered with lace doilies. The trays can be arranged on one large table or scattered around the room. The advantage of the latter is that it will help your guests get to know each other as they cluster around the food.

Here are a few party snack and appetizer ideas.

PARTY SNACKS

Apricot Nut Surprise

1 lb. dried apricots	3 oz. softened cream cheese
1 tbs. finely chopped nuts	2 tbs. lemon-flavored yogurt
1 tsp. lemon juice	1 tbs. confectioners sugar

Whip together the cream cheese, yogurt, lemon juice, and confectioners sugar. Fold in the chopped nuts. Use a sharp knife to cut a pocket in each apricot. Fill each apricot with one teaspoon of the filling. Refrigerate for at least an hour and sprinkle with confectioners sugar before serving. (60 servings)

Jalapeno Pinto Pinwheels

1 8 oz. pkg. cream cheese	1 c. shredded Monterey Jack cheese
1/3 c. finely chopped red onion	1 c. sour cream
½ tsp. seasoned salt	2 finely chopped jalapeno peppers
1/8 tsp. garlic power	15 oz. can pinto beans, drained
¼ c. chopped pimentos	½ c. chopped black olives
5 large flour tortillas	1 sm. bottle chunky salsa

Blend everything together except the beans and tortillas. Cover and refrigerate for at least three hours. Whip beans in a food processor until smooth. Spread each tortilla with a thin layer of beans, covered with a thin layer of the refrigerated mixture. Roll up the tortillas tightly, wrap in foil and refrigerate for one hour. Cut into one-inch slices and serve "pinwheel" side up on plate garnished with salsa. (15 servings)

Parmesan Mushrooms

3 lbs. large fresh mushrooms	6 tbs. extra virgin olive oil
¾ c. finely chopped scallions	2 c. finely chopped red bell
½ c. no-fat mayonnaise	pepper
1 tbs. red wine	¼ c. Dijon mustard
1 tsp. garlic powder	1 tsp. dried oregano
4 tbs. grated Parmesan cheese	

Remove mushroom stems. Roll mushrooms in oil and broil (caps right side up) for 6 to 8 minutes until tender. Chop the mushroom stems and add to the onions and bell pepper; saute in oil for 4 minutes; add wine and saute for another minute. Add the mayonnaise and mustard. Stir mixture well and spoon one teaspoonful into each mushroom cap. Sprinkle with the Parmesan cheese and broil until brown. (12 servings)

Party Gorp

If you want an irresistible snack that's easy to prepare, mix these ingredients together and serve in bowls or baskets:

Peanuts	Raisins
M&Ms	Sunflower seeds

Chopped dates   Chocolate chips
Crumbled Heath bars (tap them with
     a hammer while still in wrapper)

Snack Mix

1 box Wheat Chex	1 box Rice Chex
1 box Corn Chex	1 lg. can mixed nuts
1 lg. jar peanuts	1 pkg. thin pretzels
1 lb. butter	2 tbs. chili powder
1 tbs. onion salt	¼ c. Worcestershire sauce

Pour the cereals, nuts and pretzels into a flat metal baking pan. Melt butter and seasonings together over a low heat. Pour over the cereal/nut mixture and bake in 250 degree oven for 45 minutes.

CHIPS 'N DIPS

Along with any kind of sturdy chips, serve one or more of these homemade dips.

Guacamole

4 ripe avocados	16 oz. low-fat cottage cheese
¾ c. chopped green onions	½ c. jalapeno pepper slices, drained
¼ c. lemon juice	2 cloves garlic
2 tsp. chili powder	½ c. chopped tomato
8 sliced black olives	Salsa

Save about half of the onions, chopped tomatoes, and olives; blend the rest with the remaining ingredients in a blender or food processor until smooth, adding salsa until the mixture is soft enough to be dipped without breaking the chips. Scoop the mixture into a bowl and garnish with remaining onions, tomatoes, and olives. (12 servings)

Horseradish Crab Dip

2½ c. imitation crab meat, shredded
3 8-oz. packages Neufchâtel cream cheese, softened
1½ c. undiluted evaporated skimmed milk

½ c. finely sliced green onions
½ c. finely chopped red bell pepper
1 tsp. garlic salt
2 tsp. prepared horseradish

Whip the milk and cream cheese together; stir in the rest of the ingredients. Cover and refrigerate for two hours. (Makes 6 cups.)

Creamy Spinach Dip in a Bread Bowl

3 large round sourdough loaves of French bread
4 c. low fat yogurt
2 10-oz. pkgs. frozen chopped spinach, thawed and squeezed dry
½ c. reduced-calorie mayonnaise
2 pkgs. dry onion soup mix

Mix together the yogurt, spinach, mayonnaise, and onion soup mix; cover and chill in the refrigerator for up to 4 hours. Use a sharp knife to hollow out the loaves of French bread. Fill the bread "bowls" with the spinach mixture and serve with the scooped-out bread pieces, which can be used as dippers.(20 servings)

Cilantro Bean Dip

2 cans drained black beans
1 c. low fat sour cream
¼ c. chopped cilantro
1 tsp. garlic powder
1 c. non-fat mayonnaise
2 tsp. hot sauce
2 tsp. chili powder
2 4-oz. cans chopped green chilies, drained

Mash beans with a fork or use a food processor at slow speed. Mix in remaining ingredients, cover and refrigerate for one hour. (Makes 5 cups.)

Clam Cocktail Dip

4 c. low fat sour cream
3 6¼-oz. cans minced clams, drained
½ c. chopped green onions (save about half)
¼ c. Worcestershire sauce
½ tsp. black pepper

Set aside half of the onions and mix the remaining ingredients together. Chill in the refrigerator for at least two hours. Serve in a brightly colored bowl. Add remaining onions as garnish. (Makes approximately 4 cups.)

EASY APPETIZERS

Strawberry Ring. Arrange large fresh strawberries in a ring around a bowl of confectioners sugar for dipping.

Shrimp Cocktail. Arrange large cooked shrimp in a ring around a bowl of cocktail sauce.

Oysters on the Half Shell. Wash oysters in shells. Chill. Open. Arrange halves on a plate of crushed ice in a ring around a bowl of cocktail sauce.

Broiled Cocktail Sausages. Cut a cabbage into two halves and place cut-side down on two plates. Broil cocktail sausages. Skewer them with long wooden or plastic party picks and stick them into the cabbages, capping each pick with a black olive.

Ham and Cream Cheese Rolls. Spread thin ham slices with pineapple-cream cheese. Roll and skewer with short plastic party picks.

Note: You may also want to consider serving Mexican Nachos or Swedish Meatballs. See Chapter 12 for recipes.

Chapter 12

Party Meals

If your party calls for a full meal, as opposed to lighter fare such as appetizers or dessert, this chapter includes a variety of choices, including breakfast and luncheon buffets, a formal tea party or sit-down dinner, plus international menus. The rule, however, is that if a *knife* is required in order to eat the meal, it *must* be a sit-down affair.

As you read over the various menus, keep in mind your theme, budget and your "threshold of pain" when it comes to preparation. As to the latter, many experts recommend that, unless you're accustomed to entertaining large crowds in your home, you'll probably find that 25 to 30 people are the most you can handle for a full meal if you're doing all the work yourself.

Of course, if you're bringing in deli foods, hiring a caterer, or receiving a little help from your friends, you may be able to handle more than 30 guests.

Another thing to think about as you read through the recipes is that none of the menus are set in stone. Just because the "tea sandwiches" are suggested as part of the Alice in Wonderland Tea Party, there's no rule that says they can't be served for a sit-down or buffet luncheon.

The following recipes have been party-tested and are sure to please!

INFORMAL PARTY CUISINE

Bundle-of-Joy Breakfast Buffet

A note regarding buffets, breakfast, or otherwise: The latest trend is to serve food from several food stations, as opposed to the traditional buffet table. In the case of the breakfast buffet, for example, this would mean that hot dishes would be served from one station, pastries and fruit from another, and drinks from yet another. Guests seem to prefer this arrangement because they can "get at the food" faster, and hostesses like it better because it makes the food "look like more."

If you decide to go with one long table, you may want to stack the plates on both sides, encouraging your guests to form two lines instead of one. Place two serving spoons in each dish, one facing each side of the table. In any case, be sure the napkins and utensils are at the end of the table or at the last food station. This will give your guests one less thing to juggle as they fill their plates with food.

The Stork's Favorite Breakfast

Bacon, ham, or sausage
Scrambled eggs
Hot buttered biscuits
Heated Danish pastries
Orange juice
Bowl of fresh strawberries, raspberries, or boysenberries
Coffee, tea

Humpty Dumpty Pancake or Waffle Breakfast

Bacon, ham, or sausage
Pancakes or waffles
Assorted syrups: warm maple and blueberry and boysenberry
Orange juice
Bowl of fresh strawberries, raspberries, or boysenberries
Coffee, tea

Note: For a more formal breakfast, see "Champagne Breakfast" later in this chapter.

Mother Goose's Luncheon Buffet

Again, you can serve your luncheon buffet from one long table or several food stations.

Jack and Jill's Antipasto Tray

    8 oz. of sliced oven-roasted turkey breast
    1 large can jumbo pitted black olives, drained
    8 oz. sliced salami
    8 oz. sliced prosciutto
    8 oz. Provolone cheese slices
    8 oz. of jalapeno Monterey Jack cheese, cut into 1-inch cubes
    6-oz. jar of pimento-stuffed green olives, drained
    Deviled eggs topped with anchovies
    Marinated mushrooms
    Cherry tomatoes, radishes, and scallions
    Celery stuffed with chicken salad, cream cheese, deviled ham, or
        prepared cheese spreads
    1 7-oz. jar of baby corn cobs, drained
    3 6-oz. jars of marinated artichoke hearts, drained
    Bread sticks

Place a glass or mug in the middle of a large, circular tray and fill it with the bread sticks. Arrange the rest of the ingredients on the tray and serve. (24 servings)

Little Bo-Peep's Sandwich Potpourri

    40 slices of party rye
    40 small endive or butter lettuce leaves
    1 lg. can tuna, drained and flaked
    ½ lb. frozen cooked bay shrimp, thawed
    ½ med. cucumber, thinly sliced
    1 c. non-fat mayonnaise
    ¼ c. Dijon mustard

Add a few of the following:

Pimento strips
Caviar
Sliced green onions
Small tomato slices
Jumbo, pitted black olives, sliced in half
Steamed, fresh asparagus tips
Steamed, frozen pea pods
Dill sprigs

Lay out the bread and crackers and begin decorating with the ingredients listed above. First, moisten with mayo and/or mustard and then lay two or three ingredients on each, being as creative as possible so that each one looks different. To show them off, arrange them on the darkest tray you can find—preferably black. (40 servings)

Old King Cole's Fresh Fruit Tray

Any fresh fruit will work, although strawberries, melons and grapes are popular choices because they hold up well and have a showy appearance.

Little Jack Horner's Rainbow Slaw

4 c. shredded cabbage	½ c. chopped bell pepper
1 lg. can sliced peaches, drained	1 c. chopped celery
1½ c. miniature marshmallows	Mayonnaise to moisten

Combine ingredients, mix well, and chill.(10 servings)

Wee Willie Winkie's Waldorf Salad

4 c. diced Red Delicious apples	2 tbs. sugar
2 c. diced celery	1 tsp. lemon juice
2 c. walnut pieces	Dash of salt
½ c. mayonnaise	1 c. whipped cream

Mix together the mayonnaise, sugar, lemon juice, whipped cream and salt. Add apples, celery, and walnuts and chill. (12 servings)

Miss Muffet's Potato Salad Surprise

12 extra-lg. chilled tomatoes	2 tsp. salt
12 med. potatoes	½ tsp. pepper
½ c. finely chopped red onion	½ c. Italian salad dressing
1 c. chopped celery	1 c. mayonnaise
4 hard-boiled eggs, cut up	2 tbs. mustard
1 head red leaf lettuce	1 small can sliced ripe olives

Boil potatoes in salted water until tender. Drain, cool, and peel. Cut potatoes into small cubes. Combine with onion, celery, and eggs. Combine salad dressing, mayonnaise, mustard, salt, and pepper and add to potato mixture. Cover and refrigerate for three to four hours. Cut off stem ends of chilled tomatoes to give them flat bottoms for stability. With cut side down, cut each tomato into sixths, cutting through within half an inch of the bottom. *Carefully* spread the sections apart, forming a "flower." Fill tomatoes with chilled potato mixture, top with olives, and serve on a large platter lined with red leaf lettuce.

Old Mother Hubbard's Tossed Green Salad

Tear your favorite lettuce into bite-sized pieces and combine with sliced tomatoes, green onions, artichoke hearts, fresh sliced mushrooms, canned garbanzo beans, and slices of avocado. Serve with a variety of dressings on the side.

Note: Several of the Snack and Appetizer ideas mentioned in Chapter 11 may also be added to your luncheon buffet, such as Apricot Nut Surprise, Jalapeno Pinto Pinwheels, or any of the Easy Appetizers. Many of the international dishes found later in this chapter can also be part of your luncheon buffet, whether your party has an ethnic theme or not.

Captain Cook's Favorite Luau

In doing research for this book, I found the luau to be the most popular party theme of all. I don't know if this is because it reminds people of carefree Hawaiian vacations they've taken, or if it just seems like a festive "hang-loose" kind of party.

In addition to your decorations, a creative food display will add to the luau's ambience. By the way, a luau is one of those meals that *should* be served from one table. Here are a few of the items usually served at a luau:

♦ Roast pork.
♦ Grilled fish.
♦ Fresh pineapple slices, soaked in teriyaki sauce and lightly grilled.
♦ Fresh strawberries.
♦ Fresh melons.
♦ Papayas.
♦ Roasted bananas (peel, dip in melted butter and sprinkle with sugar; wrap in aluminum foil and roast for 20 minutes; serve with a drizzle of rum).
♦ Sweet Hawaiian bread.
♦ Bowls of sweet, fresh coconut.
♦ Boiled sweet potatoes.
♦ Fresh green salad with tomatoes, onions, raw zucchini squash, cucumbers and plenty of ripe avocados.
♦ Hawaiian fruit salad (see below).
♦ Bowls of Macadamia nuts.
♦ Of course, a bowl of poi. (Poi is that stuff that everyone says tastes like wallpaper paste. I think it tastes like nothing, and yet it's a *must* for any luau, as a conversation piece if nothing else!)

Hawaiian fruit salad

1 c. sour cream	1 c. shredded coconut
1 c. pineapple bits, drained	1½ c. miniature marshmallows
1½ c. Mandarin oranges, drained	Freshly ground nutmeg

Combine all ingredients except the nutmeg and let chill in refrigerator overnight. Sprinkle with the nutmeg just before serving.

Little Cowboy or Cowgirl Barbecue

In addition to the usual hot dogs, hamburgers, steaks, chicken, or turkey fillets, here are a few interesting alternatives:

Home on the Range Kabobs

3 lbs. lean round steak	3 red bell peppers
3 green bell peppers	1½ cups steak sauce
4 cloves garlic	2 c. beer
2 tsp. cornstarch	2 tsp. ground cumin

Crush the garlic and add it to the beer, steak sauce, and cumin; stir well. Cut the round steak into ¾ inch strips, place in a glass bowl and cover with the garlic-beer marinade. Refrigerate for three to four hours. Remove steak from the marinade (save the marinade). Cut the bell peppers into 2-inch pieces. Thread the steak and pepper pieces alternately onto 12 skewers (leave space between each piece). Place the remaining marinade in a pan, add the cornstarch and bring to a boil. Place the kabobs on the grill and cook for approximately 15 minutes, turning and brushing with marinade frequently.

Note: If you don't have barbecue skewers, you can use heavy-duty wire coat hangers. (12 servings)

Husky Corn on the Cob

Soak the corn (husk and all) in water for about 15 minutes. Then lay the corn, still in its husks, over the coals for about 20 minutes, turning constantly.

Roasted Southwest Potatoes

Split potatoes, sprinkle with garlic salt, and spray with butter-flavored oil. Wrap in heavy-duty foil and place over very hot coals for about 30 minutes.

Paul Bunyan's Hearty Favorites

What men really want when they're hungry is something hearty and filling—something "man-sized." Of course, men always like a barbecue, especially when steaks are involved, and they can usually get their fill at a pasta party, but here are a few more favorites to consider.

"Lumberjack" Pizza

Call your favorite pizzeria and order pies with a variety of toppings. Have it delivered, of course! That way, you'll only need to add a giant tossed salad and a dessert.

Blue Ox Reuben Sandwiches

Black rye bread	Swiss cheese
Corned beef, cooked & sliced	Canned sauerkraut
Butter	Thousand Island dressing
Hot mustard	

For each sandwich, butter all sides of two pieces of bread. On inside of sandwich, spread hot mustard on one piece of bread and the dressing on the other. Drain sauerkraut well. Place a layer of corned beef, a layer of sauerkraut and a layer of Swiss cheese. Grill sandwich on medium heat until cheese is melted.

Potato Salad

Use the potato salad surprise recipe under "Luncheon Buffet" or the Hot German Potato Salad recipe found later in this chapter.

Tall-Tale Chili

Make it easy on yourself by purchasing the giant-sized cans of Dennison's hot chili con carne. (I've tried and I can't make it any better from scratch!)

Hungry Man Hamburger Pie

Trust me—men love this!

2 lbs. ground round	2 cans condensed tomato soup
2 onions, chopped	10 boiled potatoes, mashed
1 tsp. salt	1 c. warm milk
½ tsp. pepper	2 cans cut green beans, drained
2 eggs, beaten	1 c. grated cheddar cheese
Two baked pie shells	

In a large skillet cook meat and onion until meat is brown and onion is tender. Add salt and pepper. Add drained beans and soup. Pour mixture into the pie shells. Mash potatoes while they are still hot; add milk and eggs. Spoon mounds of mashed potatoes over the meat mixture. Sprinkle potatoes with the grated cheese. Bake at 350 degrees for about 25 minutes. (8 man-sized servings)

Tip: Any meal that is served buffet style will require lap trays or small tables nearby for the guests to rest their drinks and silverware as they eat. It is almost impossible to juggle a plate of food, a drink and utensils while standing, unless all the foods can be eaten with the fingers, such as appetizers or snack-type finger foods.

FORMAL PARTY CUISINE

Cinderella's Champagne Breakfast

A champagne breakfast is more formal than either of the two breakfast buffets described earlier in this chapter. It will require your finest linen tablecloth and napkins, china, crystal, and silver service, champagne flutes and a silver wine cooler, if available. Here is a suggested menu:

- ♦ Chilled tomato and orange juice.
- ♦ Canadian bacon.
- ♦ Scrambled eggs with sauteed mushrooms and green onions (add one tablespoon of cream per egg).
- ♦ Large fresh strawberries with freshly whipped cream.
- ♦ Thinly sliced nut, banana, orange and raisin breads, with butter and cream cheese.
- ♦ Hot croissant rolls with berry preserves.
- ♦ Regular coffee, specialty coffees (see Chp. 13) and, of course, chilled champagne.

Alice in Wonderland Tea Party

The most common time for a tea party is on a weekend afternoon around two, usually on a Saturday. Although you may choose to host such an elegant affair, there is no reason for it to be "starched" or "stuffy." A tea party is considered a formal event, but it can still be an enjoyable, relaxed time for your guests. It all depends on you. You, as hostess, can set the tone for the afternoon with a gentle, gracious, relaxed attitude.

Tea parties actually originated in England, so the cuisine has a distinctive British flair. Let's begin with the most important thing of all—the tea itself.

Alice's Proper Tea

The secret to an excellent cup of tea is to start with cold water, which you bring to a full boil. Meanwhile, pre-warm the teapot by filling it with hot water from the tap. It is impractical to keep repeating this process if you have a large group, so keep a large carafe of hot water available.

There are all kinds of teas you can serve: herbal, black, spiced, orange pekoe, and, of course, hundreds of scented and blended teas, each with their own exotic brand names. A liqueur may also be added, such as Grand Marnier, Amaretto, Creme de Menthe, and Frangelico. As hostess, you may serve any tea of your choice.

The Mad Hatter's Favorite Tea Sandwiches

These sandwiches differ from the party sandwiches described earlier in this chapter in that they are smaller, fancier, and more time-consuming to put together. Start with thinly-sliced breads, such as rye, pumpernickel, or any of the "diet breads" on the market. Instead of mayonnaise and mustard, these delicate finger sandwiches start with softened butter, which will keep the fillings from making the bread soggy.

Step 1: Cover each piece of bread with butter.
Step 2: Make the sandwiches using any of the fillings suggested below.

Step 3: Shortly before serving, remove from the refrigerator, trim off the crusts and cut into shapes: rectangles; triangles; squares; rounds, hearts and any other fancy shape that can be cut with a cookie cutter. (The bread cuts cleanly when cold.)

Here are some of the most popular fillings, but always remember to butter the bread first, regardless of what other garnishes may be added.

Ham and Swiss. Thinly sliced ham and Swiss cheese slices, garnished with Dijon mustard.

Turkey and cranberry. Thinly sliced turkey, garnished with a mixture of whole cranberry sauce and Dijon mustard.

Salmon and cream cheese. A layer of softened cream cheese (thinned with cream and fresh dill) and a thin layer of smoked salmon.

Egg and black olive. A filling made from 8 hard-boiled eggs that have been crumbled and mixed with ¼ cup mayonnaise, ¼ cup plain yogurt, 3 teaspoons curry powder, and one small can of chopped black olives.

Walnuts and cream cheese. A mixture of one package softened cream cheese, whipped until smooth with ¼ cup cream. Then add ½ cup finely-diced celery and ½ cup chopped almonds or walnuts.

Pineapple and cream cheese. A mixture of one package softened cream cheese, whipped until smooth with ¼ cup cream. Then add 1 cup well-drained crushed pineapple. (This is my personal favorite, especially when served on Boston brown bread.)

Chicken and bacon. Whip butter with a splash of lemon juice, ½ teaspoon Dijon mustard, and a tablespoon of mayonnaise. Mix with chopped chicken breast and finely crumbled bacon.

Apricot and cream cheese. Mix one cup of apricot preserves with 1 cup softened cream cheese and spread on the bread. Add thinly sliced ham.

Cucumber and watercress. Now here's something *really* British! Alternate layers of thinly sliced cucumbers (sprinkled with vinegar and salt) and watercress.

Queen of Hearts' Tarts

Make your own tart shells from fillo dough (found in the frozen food section of your supermarket), or buy ready-to-use tart shells from your bakery. Fill with any kind of fruit preserve and top with freshly whipped cream.

Cheshire Cat's Delectable Scones

Scones are light, tender biscuits, best served hot from the oven.

4 c. flour	1 c. cream
2 eggs	1/3 c. butter
½ tsp. salt	½ c. sugar
1½ tbs. baking powder	

Sift the dry ingredients together and cut in butter until crumbly. Add the eggs and cream. Knead the dough for about 45 seconds. Roll out ½ inch thick and cut into triangles. Bake at 400 degrees for about 15 minutes. Serve with butter and preserves. (20 servings)

Variations: Add raisins, berries, molasses, nuts, or dried currants.

Tip: If you don't want to do all the work of making scones from scratch, pick up a box of scone mix from the supermarket. (I won't tell!)

The March Hare's Dream Puffs

1 c. flour	4 eggs
½ c. softened butter	1 c. water
¼ c. sugar (optional)	½ tsp. salt

Combine water and butter in a saucepan and bring to a boil. Remove from heat and add the flour, sugar, and salt all at once. Stir quickly, forming mixture into a thick, smooth ball. Beat the eggs together thoroughly and add to the ball, a little at a time. Spoon the dough about 2 inches apart onto greased cookie sheets. Bake at 400 degrees for about 10 minutes, then at 350 degrees for 10 more minutes, until crisp.

Fill with chicken, tuna or shrimp salad, mincemeat pie mix, or any canned fruit pie filling. (25 servings)

Tip: You can save a lot of work by purchasing ready-to-use frozen puff pastry in your supermarket.

Prince Charming's Formal Sit-Down Dinner

Although informality is the trend in baby showers, a sit-down dinner may be preferable for a formal co-ed party. If you like the idea of a formal dinner, but you'd rather not prepare and serve it yourself, you may decide to have it catered so you can relax and enjoy the occasion. However, if you do decide to prepare and serve the dinner yourself, here is an elegant menu that includes several dishes that can be prepared in advance, which will ease a little of the last minute anxiety.

Appetizers

Select from the Snack and Appetizer menu in Chapter 11.

Vichyssoise

This elegant French soup is actually quite easy to prepare if you use instant potatoes (no one will ever know!). And, of course, it can be cooked ahead of time and left in your refrigerator until served.

    2 sm. yellow onions, grated
    2 tbs. instant chicken bouillon
    2 c. water
    ½ tsp. salt
    4 c. whole milk
    2½ c. instant dry mashed potatoes
    2 c. heavy cream
    Chopped chives

Combine onion, bouillon, water, and salt in large kettle. Heat to boiling. Reduce heat, cover and simmer for 15 minutes. Remove from heat. Add milk and instant potatoes. Whip until fluffy. Gradually stir in remaining milk and heat *just* to boiling point. Cover and chill in refrigerator.

Just before serving, stir in the heavy cream, beating vigorously with a fork until blended. Serve topped with chopped chives. (12 servings)

Grapefruit, Melon, Avocado Salad

2 lg. Crenshaw melons or cantaloupe
3 lg. ripe avocados
2 cans grapefruit pieces
1 c. mayonnaise
1 tbs. sugar
Orange juice, as required to thin mayonnaise
2 heads butter lettuce

Place lettuce leaves on salad plates. Cut melon slices into one-inch wide half-moon shapes and arrange three slices on each plate. Drain grapefruit and arrange pieces next to melons. Cover with plastic wrap and chill in refrigerator until ready to serve. Combine mayonnaise, sugar and enough orange juice to form a thin dressing. Chill dressing until ready to serve. Just before serving, slice each avocado into eight half-moon pieces and arrange two pieces per plate next to the grapefruit. Drizzle dressing over the salad before serving. (12 servings)

Fillet of Beef with Mushroom Sauce

6 lbs. tenderloin of beef
1 lb. bacon

Place bacon strips on top of beef and roast at 325 degrees for approximately 2½ hours (until internal meat thermometer reads 170 degrees). Cut into thick slices to serve.

Mushroom sauce: Add 1 pound of fresh, sliced sauteed mushrooms to 1 large bottle of mushroom sauce. Heat thoroughly and pour over top of beef before serving. (12 servings)

Buttered Red Potatoes

> 12 sm. red potatoes, peeled and quartered
> ½ c. melted butter
> Chopped parsley

Boil potatoes until tender. Serve covered with butter and parsley. (12 servings)

Asparagus Tips with Hollandaise Sauce

> 3 lbs. frozen asparagus tips
> 2 bottles Hollandaise sauce

This elegant dish is so easy it's embarrassing! Cook asparagus according to directions on the package. Pour the Hollandaise into your prettiest gravy server and drizzle over asparagus as it is served onto guests' plates. (12 servings)

Parker House Rolls

Purchase from your local bakery. Heat before serving.

Dessert

Serve "Bluebeard's Blueberry Surprise" (Chp. 14), but without the melon, since the guests have already had melon in their salads. However, delicate pirouette cookies may be placed in the side of the ice cream or yogurt for a dramatic touch.

Dessert Cheeses

Once the dessert has been served, bring out a tray of dessert cheeses, such as French Brie, American Liederkranz, American Camembert, Gouda, Edam, and Gruyere.

After-Dinner Mints and Chocolate Truffles

Visit your local gourmet candy store and splurge on melt-in-the-mouth mints and truffles.

Tip: If you really want to impress your guests, present the main course on an elegantly decorated serving cart that can be rolled up to each guest for French service. (French Service is when each plate is individually served off a rolling cart in the presence of the guests, as opposed to plate service, where the plates are filled in the kitchen and then brought out.)

An alternative to a formal sit-down dinner might be a "Scandinavian Smorgasbord," which is described later in this chapter. Depending on the setting and the hour of day, it can be quite a formal affair.

INTERNATIONAL PARTY CUISINE

Food stations may be used to serve any of the international menus described below, except the Scandinavian Smorgasbord, which should always be served from one long table.

Italian Feast

There are two easy ways to host an Italian pasta feast. The first is to make it a potluck, asking each guest to bring one hot pasta dish, such as spaghetti, fetuccini, ravioli, cannelloni, lasagna, or stuffed manicotti. All you'll need to provide are an antipasto tray, a green salad, and toasted garlic bread.

Or you can host your own pasta bar that features spaghetti and fettucini noodles, plus ready-made specialty sauces by Five Brothers, Prego, or Classico.

Serve each sauce in its own bowl, with a card propped in front identifying the name of the sauce. Your guests will never know you purchased these ready-made sauces at your supermarket—unless you tell them, of course!

Be sure to serve several types of grated cheeses as well, such as Parmesan, Romano, garlic herb, and zesty red pepper.

You'll also need to add a salad and garlic bread.

Scandinavian Smorgasbord

This smorgasbord is suitable for a formal or informal affair. Entrees may include:

- Swedish meatballs.
- Marinated herring with sour cream sauce.
- Marinated anchovy fillets.
- Potato sausage ("korv").
- Fish balls.
- Potato casserole.
- Deviled eggs.
- Light and dark dessert breads.
- A bowl of fruit balls and berries.
- Havarti cheese.
- Swedish paddy cakes.

The recipes for the Swedish meatballs, fish balls, and potato casserole are given below. The recipe for Swedish Paddy Cakes can be found in Chapter 14. The herring and anchovy fillets are sold in the supermarket, although you may want to add a little more sour cream, a squirt of lemon, and a few capers to the marinated herring before serving. The potato sausage can be ordered from most delicatessens. Traditionally, the fish foods are set at one end of the table and the meats at the other, with the other dishes arranged in between.

Swedish Meatballs

2 lbs. ground chuck	½ c. butter
1 lb. ground pork	2 med. yellow onions, minced
2 eggs, slightly beaten	½ tsp. nutmeg
2 tbs. cornstarch	½ tsp. ground ginger
1 c. hot milk	3 tsp. salt
2 tbs. flour	¼ tsp. allspice
1 tsp. pepper	

Mix meat, eggs, milk, and cornstarch together. Add all the rest of the ingredients, except for the flour and butter. Form mixture into small balls and brown in the butter. Add a little water and simmer slowly for about 40 minutes. Remove the meatballs from the pan and make a gravy out of the drippings by adding the flour and enough water for a medium thick gravy. (20 servings)

Fish Balls

4 lbs. salmon	½ tsp. nutmeg
1 tsp. salt	½ tsp. mace
1 tsp. pepper	Milk and butter as needed

Remove the bones and grind up the salmon with a meat grinder. Add seasonings and enough milk to form the mixture into balls. Fry in butter. (20 servings)

Potato Casserole

4 lbs. cooked, mashed potatoes	2 tsp. salt
2 lbs. canned Danish bacon	½ tsp. white pepper
6 med. yellow onions	4 c. cubed pickled beets
Chopped parsley	

Dice bacon and onions and saute in butter until onions are tender. Add seasonings to the mashed potatoes. Place potatoes in large casserole dish and pour the drained bacon and onions over the top. Bake in 300 degree oven for 10 minutes. Garnish with pickled beets and parsley. (20 servings)

Taste of Mexicana

Mexican Nachos

Combine shredded jack cheese and shredded cheddar cheese (3 parts jack to 1 part cheddar) and microwave on high for two minutes, stirring halfway through. Serve with large tortilla chips.

Taco Salad

2 lbs. ground beef	2 lbs. canned red kidney beans
½ tsp. salt	½ tsp. pepper
½ tsp. garlic powder	1 head lettuce, torn into small pieces
2 lg. tomatoes, cubed	3 lg. avocados, cubed
4 scallions, sliced	1 c. grated cheddar cheese
2 c. crushed tortilla chips	2 c. salsa

Brown beef and drain well. Add drained beans and seasonings and cook at low heat for five minutes. Toss together with the lettuce, tomato, avocado, scallions, cheese, and tortilla chips. Top with salsa and serve. (Serves 12 to 14)

Chili Salsa Salad

Lg. bottle medium-hot salsa
2 sm. cans corn (non-creamed)
1 med. can diced green chilies
2 tbs. lime juice
1 tbs. chili powder
Crumbled tortilla chips

Mix first five ingredients together and chill. Sprinkle with crumbled tortilla chips just before serving.

Taco Picanti Casserole

2 boxes Spanish-style Rice-a-Roni or Farmhouse Mexican style rice

4 corn tortillas	1 24-oz. jar medium-hot picanti sauce
2 lbs. extra-lean hamburger	1 15-oz. can non-fat refried beans
6 cloves of garlic, chopped	4 4-oz. cans diced green chilies
2 sm. onions, chopped	16 oz. low-fat sharp cheddar cheese
1 8-oz. can sliced black olives	2 tsp. ground cumin
2 7-oz. cans yellow corn, drained	
Scallions	

Prepare the rice according to directions on box. Spray a heavy skillet with fat-free nonstick spray, and brown hamburger with garlic, onions, and cumin. Drain well on a paper towel and combine with the rice mixture. Prepare two round glass casserole dishes with fat-free spray. Cut six tortillas into eight triangles each. Arrange eight triangles in a pie shape on the bottom of each dish, followed by layers of the beef mix, beans, whole green chilies, picanti sauce, corn, and cheese. Repeat the process, ending with a topping of eight more tortilla triangles and grated cheese. Finally, garnish with sliced black olives and chopped scallions.

Bake at 375 degrees for about 40 minutes, until it is all melted together. Let sit for 10 minutes before serving. (12-14 servings)

Tijuana Tamale Pie

1½ lbs. ground beef	2 sm. cans sliced black olives
5 c. milk	2¼ c. yellow cornmeal
4 beaten eggs	1 lb. grated Cheddar cheese
2 7-oz. cans whole kernel corn	2 tsp. garlic salt
2 tsp. chili powder	1 lg. jar medium-hot salsa

2 14½-oz cans whole peeled tomatoes, undrained and cut up
2 pkgs. Lawry's Spices & Seasonings for Chili (or Lawry's Taco Spices & Seasonings)

Brown ground beef until crumbly and drain well. In a large bowl combine milk, 2 cups cornmeal, and eggs. Add beef and remaining ingredients, except for the cheese and ¼ cup of cornmeal. Stir together and pour into two lightly greased 12" x 8" x 2" baking dishes. Bake uncovered in 350 degree oven for 40 to 45 minutes. Sprinkle with the cheese and remaining cornmeal; continue baking until cheese melts and cornmeal is browned. Let stand for 10 minutes before serving. Serve with salsa. (Serves 16)

Tip: Serve Mexican Baby Blankets for dessert (see Chp. 14).

Leprechaun's Favorite Fare

Corned Beef & Cabbage

6 lbs. well-trimmed corned beef brisket
3 cloves garlic, minced
2 sm. onions, quartered
1 lg. head green cabbage, cut into wedges
6 lg. red potatoes, peeled and quartered

Place brisket in large kettle and cover with cold water. Add garlic and onions. Heat to boiling. Reduce heat, cover tightly and simmer for four hours, or until tender. About 30 minutes before meat is tender, add potatoes to the pot. Remove the meat when it is tender, place on a hot platter and cover with foil to keep warm while you cook the cabbage. Add cabbage to the kettle and boil until cabbage and potatoes are tender, about 15 minutes. To serve, surround the brisket with the drained cabbage and potatoes. Very important: Brisket must be sliced thinly *across* the grain.

Irish Stew

6 lbs. lamb roast, cut into 1" cubes
2 c. each of cut-up carrots, turnips, celery, yellow onions

8 c. cubed potatoes	2 tsp. salt
1 tsp. pepper	2 bay leaves
¼ c. minced parsley	1 tsp. thyme
Mint leaves	

Roll meat in flour and brown in hot olive oil. Cover with boiling water and simmer for two hours. Add vegetables and seasonings and simmer 45 minutes, or until vegetables are tender. Thicken liquid for gravy. Garnish with mint leaves.

Irish Potatoes

The Irish like their potatoes "straight up," just boiled in their skins, drained and served. Small new potatoes are a favorite.

Fruit and Cheese Tray

As I mentioned earlier, any fresh fruit will work, although strawberries, melons, and grapes are popular choices because they hold up well and have a showy appearance. Also, specialty cheeses are very nice, such as French Brie, American Liederkranz, American Camembert, Gouda, Edam, and Gruyere.

Tip: Serve Blarney Stone Cobbler for dessert (see Chp. 14).

Oriental Delight

Chinese Chicken Salad

4 whole chicken breasts, cut into thin strips

Virgin olive oil	8 scallions, sliced thin
2 heads of lettuce, shredded	1 c. chopped parsley
1 tsp. dry mustard	1 tsp. sugar
½ tsp. salt	½ tsp. dry ginger
½ c. sesame seeds, toasted	1 c. slivered almonds, toasted
1/3 c. plum sauce	

Stir fry chicken strips in 2 tablespoons oil until cooked through. Allow chicken to cool. Toss lettuce, onion, and parsley together in a large salad bowl. Add cooled chicken.

Combine 4 tablespoons oil, plum sauce, mustard, sugar, and seasonings. Add to the salad, tossing gently. Garnish with sesame seeds and almonds.

Pork Chow Mein

4 c. thinly sliced lean, boneless pork
1 med. yellow onion, chopped

3 c. water	3 c. chopped celery
2 tsp. salt	2 cans bean sprouts
1/3 c. corn starch	1 tsp. pepper
2 tbs. brown sauce	¼ c. soy sauce

Spray wok or skillet with cooking spray and fry pork and onion together until tender. Add celery, salt, pepper, and water. Cook for 20 minutes. Drain. Add bean sprouts and bring to boil. Make a paste of the corn starch, soy sauce, and brown sauce and pour it over the mixture, cooking only until thickened. Serve over chow mein noodles.

Shrimp Fried Rice

3 c. cold cooked rice	2 tbs. peanut or olive oil
¼ lb. cooked shrimp	¼ c. light soy sauce
2 eggs	3 green onions, chopped
¼ c. sliced water chestnuts	½ c. peas

Blend eggs with 2 tablespoons water and set aside. Heat oil in a wok or heavy skillet over medium heat. Add green onions and stir fry for 30 seconds. Adds eggs, stirring until firm. Stir in rice and cook until heated through. Add shrimp, peas, water chestnuts, and soy sauce, stirring until blended and shrimp is heated through.

Chinese Cabbage

2 heads cabbage, shredded
½ lb. butter

Boil cabbage for five minutes. Serve topped with melted butter.

Fluffy White Rice

Prepare plain white rice and serve in large bowl.

Pot Stickers

Purchase them in bulk from the freezer section at your supermarket. They are easy to prepare—just steam them in a heavy skillet.

Note: Of course, you can always order take-out, especially if you're short on time. (That's what I *always* do!)

Oktoberfest

Lentil Soup

4 c. dried lentils	6 stalks celery, chopped
Lg. ham bone	2 sprigs parsley
2 lg. yellow onions, minced	1 tsp. each salt and pepper
¼ c. each butter and flour for thickening (if desired)	

Soak lentils in water overnight. Place lentils, ham bone, onion, celery, parsley, and seasonings in large kettle, covered by 6 quarts of water. Bring to a boil, cover and simmer for about five hours, until lentils are tender. Thicken, if desired, with ¼ cup butter and ¼ cup flour. (16 servings)

Fried Bratwurst

Purchase one bratwurst per guest. Fry the bratwurst in butter, turning frequently until golden brown on all sides. Cover the bratwurst with water and simmer uncovered for 20 minutes.

Serve with hot mustard or sour cream.

Sauerbraten

4 lbs. lean boneless top round beef steak, cut with the grain into 2-inch strips, then cut across the grain into ¼-inch-thick slanting slices.	
1 c. each dry white wine and white vinegar	
¼ c. dark brown sugar	4 dry bay leaves
1 tsp. each pepper and ground cloves	¼ c. salad oil
4 red onions, thinly sliced	4 c. thinly sliced carrots

2 c. thinly sliced celery	4 cloves garlic, minced
½ c. water	1 c. crushed gingersnaps
Sour cream (optional)	

In a bowl, mix wine, vinegar, brown sugar, bay leaf, pepper, and cloves. Stir in meat and let marinate for one hour. Drain meat, reserving marinade. Remove bay leaves.

Place wok or heavy skillet over high heat. Add oil. When oil is hot, add meat and stir fry until meat is browned (about two minutes). Remove meat and add onion and carrots. Stir fry for one minute. Add celery and garlic. Stir fry for one minute. Add water, cover and cook until carrots and celery are tender, about three more minutes.

Return meat to wok and add marinade and gingersnaps. Stir until sauce thickens. Serve garnished with dollops of sour cream. (Serves 16)

Hot German Potato Salad

12 med. potatoes, boiled in skins, peeled and cut into thin slices.
14 slices of bacon, fried until crisp and broken into pieces

1½ c. diced yellow onion	1 tsp. celery seed
¼ c. flour	1 tsp. pepper
¼ c. sugar	1½ c. water
3 tsp. salt	1 c. vinegar
1 tbs. chopped chives	

Cook onion in bacon fat. Mix in all dry ingredients. Add water and vinegar and cook until mixture boils. Simmer for three minutes. Pour over potatoes. Add most of the bacon pieces. Cover and let stand until ready to serve. Garnish with remaining bacon and minced chives. (Serves 12)

Sauerkraut

Purchase canned or fresh deli sauerkraut.

Fruit and Cheese Tray

(Described under "Leprechaun's Favorite Fare" on page 134.)

Chapter 13

Party Drinks

You may choose to serve a selection of wines, soft drinks, coffee, or tea. But if you'd like to jazz up your party with some popular new party drinks, this chapter includes your choice of smoothies, specialty fruit drinks, punch recipes, and specialty coffee drinks.

CALIFORNIA SMOOTHIES

Smoothies are a frosty-cold blend of fruits, juices, and yogurt or sorbet that are prepared in a blender. A smoothie is considered to be healthier than a milkshake and more substantial than a lemonade— the trendy new drink of the decade. *Newsweek* magazine, in fact, has declared it to be the "new cool brew" and predicts it will become as popular as specialty coffees.

In addition to the basics listed above, "smoothie chefs" customize their recipes with almost anything you can think of—from brownies to tofu. The ingredients listed in each of the smoothie recipes below should be blended together to make one large smoothie.

The Inner Child Smoothie

1 c. frozen vanilla yogurt
½ c. peanut butter
½ c. apple juice
½ c. honey

Pink Princess

1 c. frozen strawberry yogurt
1 banana
½ c. fresh strawberries
1 c. orange juice

Mad Hatter's Zinger

1 cucumber, peeled, seeded, and chopped
2 tbs. finely chopped mint leaves
1 c. apple cider
1 c. lemon sorbet
½ c. crushed ice

Malibu Tango

8 apricots, pitted and chopped
½ c. frozen vanilla yogurt
3 sm. peeled, sliced tangerines
1 tbs. sugar

Papaya Pleasure

1 c. peeled, seeded, and chopped cantaloupe
1 c. freshly squeezed orange juice
1 papaya, peeled, seeded, and chopped
½ c. frozen vanilla yogurt

Goes-Down-Easy Mango

1 chilled mango, peeled and chopped
1½ c. frozen vanilla yogurt
1 c. chilled fresh pineapple chunks
1 tsp. ground cardamom
½ c. crushed ice

Too-Good-to-Believe Berry

1 c. frozen vanilla yogurt
1 c. raspberries
1 c. blackberries
½ c. apple juice

Tip: Garnish your smoothies with a wedge of orange or lime, or a slice of pineapple, peach, or mango.

FESTIVE FRUIT DRINKS

Peachy Pleasure

¾ c. peach nectar	1 tbs. lime juice
3 tbs. grenadine syrup	1½ c. ice
1 Alberta peach, pitted and sliced (do not peel)	

Process the ice, nectar, peach slices, and lime juice in a juicer. Pour grenadine into bottom of each glass. Pour blended mixture on top. (Syrup will send brilliant streaks to the top of the glass, creating a "peachy sunset.")

Slushie Slurpie

2 lg. apples, cut into wedges	2½ c. blackberries
1½ c. blueberries	Whipped cream

Process the three fruits in a juicer and serve with a dollop of whipped cream on top.

Wee Bit o' Shamrock

1½ c. Thompson seedless green grapes
2 pears, cut into wedges   3 plums, pitted and cut into wedges

Process the fruits in a juicer. Garnish with a slice of lime.

Southwestern Adventure

4 lg. tomatoes, cut into wedges
1 med. cucumber, peeled and cut into wedges

3 jalapeno peppers, stemmed	2 tsp. horseradish
2 tsp. Worcestershire sauce	1 tsp. celery salt

Process all the ingredients together in a juicer and serve.

Strawberry Blast

Half a small cantaloupe, peeled and chopped
12 lg. strawberries   1 sm. apple, cut into wedges
Whipped cream

Process the strawberries, cantaloupe, and apple together in a juicer. Serve topped with whipped cream.

Cow Jumped Over the Moonbeam

½ honeydew melon, peeled, seeded, and chopped
1 apricot and 2 peaches, pitted and chopped
1 c. ginger ale

Blend the fruits together until smooth. Add the ginger ale and mix very gently.

Polynesian Breeze

3 mangoes, peeled, pitted and cut into wedges
1 c. chopped, fresh pineapple
1 c. raspberries

Process fruits together in a juicer.

Kiwi Silk

2 kiwi, peeled and cut into wedges
1 lg. peach, pitted and cut into wedges
1 c. freshly squeezed grapefruit juice
¼ c. freshly squeezed lime juice

Process the kiwi and peach in a juicer. Add grapefruit and lime juice and mix well.

Tip: Garnish your fruit drinks with a sprig of mint, a wedge of orange or lime, or a slice of pineapple, peach, or mango.

"PLEASED AS PUNCH" RECIPES

Here are a few popular new punch recipes to consider:

Sangria Punch

1 gal. red wine
½ lemon, sliced
1½ c. sugar
1 c. light rum

4 oranges, sliced and quartered
4 apples, peeled, cored, and sliced
2 tbs. cinnamon

Mix ingredients together in a large crock, or glass or plastic container and store overnight in a cool place. Do not refrigerate. Add ice just before serving.

Humpty Dumpty's Nog

12 egg yolks	1 lb. powdered sugar
1 qt. dark rum or brandy	2½ qts. whipping cream
1 qt. whole milk	6 egg whites
½ tsp. salt	Freshly grated nutmeg

Beat egg yolks until light in color. Beat in powdered sugar, cream, liquor, and milk. Cover and refrigerate for at least four hours. Beat egg whites until stiff, fold lightly with the salt, and combine with the chilled mixture.

Top each serving with freshly grated nutmeg.

Snow White's Mocha Punch

1 c. instant coffee granules	2 gal. whole milk
4 c. hot water	1 gal. vanilla ice cream
3 c. sugar	1 gal. chocolate ice cream
1 qt. whipped cream	

Combine the coffee, water, and sugar and set it in the refrigerator for one hour. Fifteen minutes before serving time, set the two gallons of ice cream out to soften. Combine one half of the cooled coffee mixture, ice cream, and milk. Spread half of the whipped cream evenly over the top of the punch and serve. (Return the rest of the ingredients to the refrigerator or freezer to use as needed to refill the punch bowl).

Wonderful Wassail

5 med. baking apples	1 c. sugar
¼ c. water	3 c. ale
3½ c. apple cider	1 tsp. allspice

Core apples and sprinkle with half a cup of sugar. Add water and bake at 375 degrees for 30 minutes, or until tender. Combine ale, cider, remaining sugar, and allspice in saucepan and place over low heat. Stir until sugar is dissolved, but do not boil. Place roasted apples in punch bowl and pour ale mixture over them.

Christmas Baby Punch

5 tea bags	5 c. boiling water
½ tsp. allspice	½ tsp. cinnamon
½ tsp. nutmeg	1 c. sugar
1 qt. cranberry juice cocktail	3 c. water
1 c. orange juice	¾ c. lemon juice

Pour boiling water over tea bags and the spices and steep for five minutes. Strain, add sugar, and let cool. Add cranberry juice cocktail, water, orange, and lemon juice and mix. Pour into punch bowl with ice cubes made from lemon juice. Float thin lemon slices on top of the punch.

Hawaiian Volcano

1 gal. cold Hawaiian fruit punch
2 c. guava juice
2 2-liter bottles cold ginger ale or lemon-lime soda
½ gal. rainbow sherbet

Mix the fruit punch and guava juice together, then add the sherbet. Pour the ginger ale or lemon-lime directly on top of the sherbet, which will make the punch foam like a "volcano."

Tip: Don't add plain ice to your punch because it will water it down. Add frozen juice instead. (Freeze the juice in circular gelatin molds or in ice cube trays.)

SPECIALTY COFFEE DRINKS

Cafe au Rhum

Add 1 ounce rum and a twist of lemon peel per cup.

Cafe Cacao

Add 1 ounce Creme de Cacao per cup.

Cafe a L'Orange

Add 1 ounce Orange Curacao per cup. Serve with a cinnamon stick for stirring.

Cafe Mocha

Equal amounts of coffee and hot chocolate topped with whipped cream.

Irish Coffee

Add one ounce Irish whiskey and 3 teaspoons of sugar. Top with whipped cream.

Cafe Cappuccino

Equal amounts of espresso (brewed from pulverized Italian dark-roast coffee) and hot milk. Add 2 teaspoons sugar and sprinkles of cinnamon and nutmeg. (Or use instant cappuccino mix instead.)

Cafe Borgia

Equal amounts of espresso and hot chocolate, served in a demitasse cup, topped with whipped cream and grated orange peel.

Coffee a la Mode

Add a couple tablespoons vanilla or coffee ice cream to the coffee just before you serve it.

Chapter 14

Party Desserts

The traditional baby shower dessert has usually been a cleverly decorated cake appropriate to the party's theme, set in the middle of the serving table as one of the party decorations. This tradition, however, is *not* set in stone. You can serve any kind of dessert you would like.

In addition to several cake ideas, this chapter includes recipes for theme-related sugar cookies and several sure-to-please baby shower desserts.

Tip: For a dramatic flare, turn the lights down low and enter the room carrying whatever dessert you choose to serve topped with lighted sparklers or sugar cubes!

DECORATED BABY SHOWER CAKES

You can order a theme-related cake from your favorite bakery, bake your own, or decorate a supermarket cake, such as a Bundt cake or an angel food cake.

Bake Your Own Cake

If you decide to make the cake yourself, you have three options:

1. Bake the cake in a standard-sized rectangular, square, or round cake pan and decorate the top of the cake, using a pattern (see the Appendix) or theme-related decorations available at a party supply store. A company by the name of Wilton Enterprises (www.wilton.com) makes hundreds of clever products, from baby shower cake pans to decorating accessories, such as a miniature train, a baby carriage, and plastic newborn babies.

2. Bake the cake in a cake pan that's already in the shape of your theme-related animal, character, or object. These cake pans are also Wilton products and are available at party supply stores or through their web site. What I love about these pans is that they come with a sized picture that shows exactly what the finished cake should look like after it has been decorated.

3. Bake the cake in rectangular, square, or round cake pans and cut the pieces to form a theme-related shape, such as a train or a teddy bear (see the Appendix).

If you decide on the latter, here are some tips:

♦ Many of the women I interviewed prefer Duncan Hines cake mixes (unless they bake the cake from scratch).

♦ It is important for your cake to be flat on top, so to prevent the cake from "mounding" in the middle as it bakes, take these two precautions:

⇨ Spread the batter from the center to the outer edges of your pan before placing in the oven.

⇨ Check the temperature of your oven to be sure it is not hotter than specified. (If the center of your oven has a "hot-spot," the batter will rise too quickly which will create a high mound in the middle of the cake.)

Tip: If your cake does mound, trim it flat before you turn it out of the pan; otherwise the cake will split as it settles.

♦ To prevent sticking or crumbling, allow your cake to cool in the pan for 10 minutes after baking—no more and no less.

♦ Use a homemade buttercream frosting made with shortening, *not* butter or margarine. This will not only prevent an off-white appearance, but will give it the proper consistency (see recipe below). Cover the cake with the frosting, reserving a portion to be used for tinting and decorating.

♦ Use paste food coloring to tint your icing—never liquid food coloring because it causes the icing to become too thin.

♦ Design your cake-top using theme-related shapes and lettering that have been drawn on paper ahead of time. You can use one of the patterns in the Appendix or copy a shape from party napkins, cards, or invitations or from a child's coloring book.

♦ Once you've decided on your design, use a toothpick to sketch it onto your cake-top. Then, using tinted frosting in a frosting cone or pastry bag with a frosting tip, just barely touch the surface as you trace over the design. If you make a mistake, use a table knife to carefully remove the icing so you can start over again.

Buttercream Frosting

This frosting can be used to frost and decorate.

Measure into a large mixing bowl:
1¼ c. shortening
1 tsp. salt
2 tsp. clear vanilla, lemon, or almond flavoring
Beat at medium speed for three minutes.

Add all at once:
2 16-oz. boxes sifted powdered sugar
9 tbs. milk or fruit juice

Beat at medium speed until frosting is the consistency of whipped cream.

DECORATE A SUPERMARKET CAKE

Ba Ba Baby Bundt Cake

    1 Bundt cake
    1 can of frosting
    1 clear glass baby bottle ("Ba Ba") with a ribbon tied at its neck

Frost the cake. Fill the baby bottle with candy and insert into the hole in the center of the cake.

Barbie Doll Cake

    1 angel food cake
    1 can of frosting
    Food coloring
    1 Barbie doll
    1 glass jar or pint-sized milk carton

Place the Barbie doll's legs into the jar or milk carton and insert in the center hole of the cake. Ice the cake with frosting to resemble a skirt. Fold the Barbie doll's real skirt over the top of the frosting "skirt."

DECORATED BABY SHOWER SUGAR COOKIES

Decorated sugar cookies are perfect for a baby shower, especially if they follow the theme, such as train cabooses or cowboy hats.

You'll find all kinds of cookie cutter shapes at your local party supply store, through Wilton's web site, or you can form your cookies by hand. For example, a teddy bear can be created with one large, one medium and six small balls of dough. Press the large ball flat to form the bear's stomach, the medium ball for its head, and the six small balls to form the four paws and two ears. Or you can cut a shape from cardboard, place it on rolled-out cookie dough and trace around the shape with a sharp knife. Of course, the quickest method is to use cookie cutter shapes.

If you don't have a favorite sugar cookie recipe, you're welcome to use mine:

Sugar Cookies

 1 c. melted butter
 1½ c. sifted confectioners sugar
 1 egg
 1½ tsp. vanilla
 2½ c. all-purpose flour, sifted
 1 tsp. baking soda
 1 tsp. cream of tartar
 Canned white frosting
 Food colorings
 ¼" ribbon

Mix the first four ingredients together thoroughly. Sift the flour, baking soda and cream of tartar together and add this mixture to the first four ingredients. Cover and chill for three hours.

Heat oven to 375 degrees. Roll the dough on a lightly floured cloth-covered board to approximately ¼-inch thickness. Cut into desired shapes and bake on lightly greased baking sheet for seven or eight minutes until lightly browned on the edges.

When the cookies are cool, frost them using the butter cream frosting recipe above, and tie them with ribbons. For example, you can tie ribbons around the bears' necks or the brims of the cowboy hats.

Tip: If you are free-forming the dough, it is not necessary to roll it out.

SPECIAL BABY SHOWER DESSERTS

Bluebeard's Blueberry Surprise

It's hard to believe that a serving of anything this delicious only has 135 calories and 2 grams of fat—but it's true!

½ gal. non-fat vanilla ice cream or frozen yogurt
3 sm. cantaloupe, thinly sliced and peeled
3 c. fresh or frozen blueberries (or raspberries or strawberries)
2½ c. orange juice
2¼ tbs. cornstarch
2/3 c. sugar

In a small saucepan stir together the sugar and cornstarch. Add the orange juice and berries. Cook and stir until mixture begins to thicken, then cook for two more minutes. Cool in refrigerator for 20 minutes. Scoop 1/3 cup ice cream or yogurt into each dessert dish. Arrange cantaloupe slices on one side of the dish. Pour berry sauce over top of ice cream or yogurt. Serve immediately. (20 servings)

Watermelon Cradle Filled with Melon Balls

Cut away half of the top of an oblong watermelon. Scoop out the watermelon pulp of half of the melon into balls (forming a "cradle" out of the melon half) and mix with two cups cantaloupe balls and two cups honeydew melon balls. Gently scoop all the melon balls into the inside of the cradle. (12 servings)

Better-than-Sex Brownies

This *definitely* has more than 135 calories and 2 grams of fat! But, what the heck!

2 19.8-oz. boxes fudge brownie mix
1 c. Kahlua
16 Heath candy bars
2 12-oz. containers whipped topping

Bake the brownies according to directions and cool. Punch holes in brownies with a fork and pour the Kahlua over the top. Tap the Heath bars with a hammer (while still in the wrapper) and crumble the pieces over the top of the soaked brownies. Top with whipped topping. (Don't worry, your guests will probably only gain 3 or 4 pounds each!)

Magic Mountain Sundaes

Serve bowls filled with scoops of various flavors of ice cream, and arrange the following toppings on a serving table so your guests can make their own sundaes.

Chocolate, hot fudge, butterscotch, caramel, or kiwi sauce (blend 3
    peeled kiwi, 3 tbs. honey, 2 tsp. lemon juice, 1 tsp. vanilla)
Strawberries, raspberries, or boysenberries
Sliced bananas, mango, kiwi, or peaches
Chopped walnuts, almonds, pecans, or peanuts
Heath, Hershey, or Butterfingers bars, crumbled
Cool Whip or fresh whipped cream

Swedish Paddy Cakes

4 c. sifted flour	1 c. sugar
2 c. softened butter	2 eggs
1 tbs. vanilla	

Cream sugar and butter together and then beat in the eggs and vanilla. Stir in the flour and mix well. Drop rounded teaspoonfuls of batter into greased tiny muffin cups, pressing batter over the bottom and up around the sides about ¼ inch thick.

Chill and then fill each hollow with almond macaroon filling.

Almond Macaroon Filling:

4 eggs	1 c. sugar
1 tsp. almond extract	3 c. finely chopped almonds

Beat eggs until foamy. Add sugar and mix until blended. Add almonds and almond extract. Pour into prepared muffin cups and bake at 325 degrees for about 25 minutes, until browned and set. (Makes 4 dozen tea cakes.)

Blarney Stone Cobbler

1½ lbs. apples	1½ lbs. blackberries
¼ c. water	1½ c. sugar
2 sticks butter	2 c. flour
1-1/3 c. oatmeal	½ c. dark brown sugar

Peel, core, and slice the apples. Add to washed blackberries and place in large, shallow baking pan. Dribble the water and sugar over the top. Combine softened butter, flour, oatmeal, and brown sugar in a bowl and mix together until the ingredients form a crumbly mixture. Evenly sprinkle these crumbly pieces over the top of the fruit, packing down lightly. Bake in preheated 400 degree oven for 15 minutes. Then reduce heat to 375 degrees and cook for another 15 to 20 minutes, or until cooked through and crunchy on top. Serve warm with whipped cream or vanilla ice cream. (16 servings)

Mexican Baby Blankets

4 c. flour	2 tsp. salt
4 tsp. baking powder	Water
¼ c. shortening	Shortening for deep frying

Sift dry ingredients together. Cut in shortening. Add just enough water to hold dough together. Roll thin and cut into 2-inch squares or triangles. Fry to a golden brown in deep, *very* hot shortening. Pastries should puff up. Serve hot with butter and honey, or sprinkle with powdered sugar.

Note: These are tricky because unless you fry them in very hot oil or shortening, they will fall flat. Try a batch ahead of time just to be sure they'll turn out okay. (12 to 15 servings)

Bambi's Berry Trifle

Now, here's a nice surprise—something that looks spectacular, but takes very little work!

2 lg. boxes of ladyfingers
Brandy or fruit liqueur
1 lg. pkg. of frozen raspberries
1 jar of apricot preserves
1 lg. pkg. of lemon pudding mix
Whipping cream
A clear glass bowl with high sides

Alternate layers of ladyfingers, drizzled with the brandy or liqueur and layers of the preserves, thawed raspberries and prepared pudding. Top with a layer of fruit piled with freshly whipped cream. Refrigerate for at least one hour. (20 servings)

Ice Cream Babies

    2 gallons strawberry ice cream
    Shredded coconut, tinted pink with food coloring
    1 tiny plastic baby per guest (six for $1.99 at party supply stores)
    White doilies

Tint the shredded coconut by shaking in a plastic bag with a few drops of red food coloring, which will turn the coconut pink. Use a large tea cup to scoop firmly packed balls of strawberry ice cream onto a cookie sheet, forming wide flat "skirts." Pack each skirt with the pink-tinted coconut. Insert one baby doll into the center of each skirt, cover with waxed paper and freeze until ready to serve. Serve on white doilies.

Baby Buggy Eclairs

    1 eclair per guest (purchase eclairs from your favorite bakery)
    Round red and white peppermint candies
    White pipe cleaners
    Tiny plastic babies
    White paper doilies

Press the peppermint candies against each eclair, creating four "wheels." Bend a single pipe cleaner to form a handle. Cut a small slit at one end of the top of the eclair. Insert a plastic doll into the eclair at the slit, its head sticking out over the "blanket." Set each eclair on a paper doily.

Dirt Pie

    1 sm. clay flower pot per guest
    1 lg. plastic drinking straw per guest
    Rocky road ice cream
    Oreo cookies
    Single-stemmed fresh flowers, preferably daisies, tulips, or daffodils

Wash flower pots well and let them dry thoroughly. Place one Oreo over the hole at the bottom of each pot. Fill each pot with rocky road ice cream to within one inch from the top. Insert a straw in the center of the ice cream and cover the ice cream with crushed Oreo cookies. Freeze until time to serve. Insert the stem of one fresh flower into each straw before serving.

Captain Hook's Cappuccino Float

Pour 3 or 4 tablespoons of chocolate syrup in the bottom of a tall clear glass. Add one crumbled cookie and one scoop of chocolate ice cream. Pour iced cappuccino* over the ice cream, to within an inch of the top of the glass. Add a small scoop of praline ice cream and a squirt of whipped cream. Serve with a cookie** stuck into the side of the praline ice cream.

*Use any instant cappuccino mix, such as General Foods International Coffees, Maxwell House, or Nescafe.
**Pepperidge Farm Chocolate Laced Pirouettes (delicate "rolled" cookies that look like tiny stovepipes).

Peter Pan's Flying Float

Vanilla ice cream
Chilled root beer
Whipped cream

This is your classic root beer float, except that you use *real* ice cream (not ice milk or low-fat ice cream), and you top it with a generous scoop of whipped cream.

Part IV

Putting It All Down on Paper

The worksheets in the following chapters have been created to help you:

♦ Know what to do and when to do it.

♦ Stay organized.

♦ Establish your party budget.

But these worksheets won't do you a bit of good if you don't use them. The biggest mistake you can make is to try to keep track of everything in your head. Take it from me: If you want the planning to be easy and successful, don't trust your memory. Although a brain isn't a computer, it *is* known to become overloaded and drop data from time to time—especially when it's under stress. So get in the habit of using these worksheets as you plan.

By the way, feel free to take these worksheets to a copy center where they can be enlarged to fit a three-ring notebook, in which you could also store several plastic zipper pouch inserts for saving receipts, sample invitations, ribbon samples, party recipes, and so forth. This notebook will be a valuable tool that will help keep you on track and make your party the easiest and most successful one you've ever hosted.

Chapter 15

The Ultimate Baby Shower Scheduler

Planning a party can seem pretty complicated at first. But once you realize that there is a logical sequence to the tasks, giving a great party will be less daunting and a lot more fun. Here are the things that usually need to be done in order to plan a baby shower:

- ◆ Decide how much time and money you have to devote to the party.
- ◆ Decide what type of party will fit within these time and budget constraints.
- ◆ Decide whether it will be in honor of the expectant mother, expectant father, both parents, or the expectant grandmother or grandfather.
- ◆ Ask around to see if anyone would like to co-host the party with you and, if so, arrange a meeting to discuss the plans.
- ◆ Ask for assistance from any friends or family members who will be willing to help out during the party (serving the food, recording the gifts, etc.).

- Talk to the guest(s) of honor to coordinate a time and date that will work best for them and other family members who will be invited (unless the shower is a surprise, of course).
- Choose a site and reserve it, if necessary.
- Decide on the number of guests and compile the guest list.
- Decide on a theme.
- Purchase or make invitations, customized for the theme, if applicable.
- Make or purchase the decorations, favors, name tags, and place cards.
- Decide which items can be rented or borrowed.
- Plan a menu and purchase or order food, cake, etc.
- Decide what type of games and activities will work best with the party's theme and the ages and profiles of the guests who will be present.

Checklists

THINGS THAT CAN BE DONE WEEKS IN ADVANCE

❑ Enlist a co-host and/or volunteers to help with the party.

❑ Confer with your guest(s) of honor regarding a convenient date and time for the party.

❑ Choose a location for the party.

❑ Choose a theme.

❑ Create or purchase invitations.

❑ Assemble a guest list; address and mail invitations. (Call the guest of honor to ask for suggestions, too.)

❑ Plan a menu, including detailed recipes and a list of food that can be prepared or purchased in advance and placed in the freezer.

❑ Place order with your deli or caterer, if applicable.

❑ Place order with your bakery (for rolls, cake, etc.).

❑ Plan the games and activities.

❑ Make or purchase favors.

❑ Make or purchase prizes.

❑ Make or purchase name tags.

❑ Make or purchase place cards.

❑ Create, purchase, borrow, or rent decorations.

❑ Purchase film or single-use cameras.

❑ Purchase and wrap your gift.

❑ Decide what you're going to wear to the party and get it ready, including hose, shoes, and accessories.

❑ Other: _____

To Be Done Two Weeks before the Party

❑ Place order with your florist, including corsage for the mother-to-be, boutonniere for the father-to-be, corsages for any mothers or grand-mothers who will be attending, plus a centerpiece and any other floral arrangements.

To Be Done One Week before the Party

❑ Call any guests who have not responded to the invitation to see if they are coming.

❑ Based on the responses to the invitations, start filling out the name tags and place cards.

❑ Wrap your own gift for the shower so that you don't forget and leave this until the day of the party!

❑ Assemble and clean all crystal, china, silver, linens, etc.

❑ If you have an ice maker, empty it frequently into plastic bags to store in your freezer. Otherwise, purchase plenty of ice ahead of time.

To Be Done a Few Days before the Party

If the party is being held in your home:

❑ Clean house.

❑ Stock the guest bathroom with hand towels, lotion, guest soaps, potpourri, a candle, etc.

❑ Call your co-host(s) and helpers to confirm their duties, including:

❑ Who will pick up orders from the florist, deli, bakery, etc.?

❑ Who will record the gifts as they are opened?

❑ Who can arrive early to help with last-minute crises?

❑ Who can arrive early to help greet the guests as they arrive?

To Be Done One or Two Days before the Party

❏ Shop for perishable food items and prepare them as far as you can ahead of time (dicing, marinating, rinsing vegetables, etc.).

❏ Pick up anything you're borrowing or renting for the party (coffee urn, punch bowl, chairs, etc.).

❏ Pick up any rented or borrowed decorations and start decorating your site.

❏ Call to confirm your floral order and the time of delivery. (Request early morning delivery on the day of the party.)

❏ Call to confirm bakery order and time it will be ready to be picked up.

❏ Call to confirm deli or catering arrangements, if applicable.

❏ Call your guest(s) of honor and any helpers to confirm their time of arrival.

❏ If the guests will be wearing coats or jackets, clear out your coat closet and fill it with empty hangers.

To Be Done the Day of the Party

❏ Last minute cooking or baking.

❏ Ask one of your helpers to pick up your bakery order.

❏ Ask one of your helpers to pick up your deli order.

❏ Ask one of your helpers to pick up any borrowed or rented decorative items.

❏ Last minute decorating, including fresh flowers for the guest bathroom and any exterior decorations.

❏ If you will be serving a sit-down meal, arrange the place cards in a clever way so the guests are forced to sit next to someone they don't know and mingle. (Be sure to separate spouses.)

❑ If you will be serving food from a buffet table, scatter TV trays around the room or provide lap trays for the guests.

❑ If you plan to serve snacks or appetizers, set them out before your guests are scheduled to arrive.

❑ Other: _____

SHOWER TIMETABLE FOR A BASIC TWO-HOUR PARTY

First 10 minutes:	Guests arrive and engage in conversation.
Next 45 minutes:	Games/activities/entertainment.
Next 30 minutes:	Guest(s) of honor opens gifts.
Final 35 minutes:	Refreshments are served.

Of course, depending on your theme, this schedule may be shuffled around, with the food being served shortly after the guests arrive, for example, especially if it is a sit-down dinner or a luncheon buffet.

HOW TO DELEGATE

Whether you ask others to co-host the party with you, or you decide to host it by yourself, you will still need help to keep things running smoothly. Here are a few of the responsibilities that can be delegated to others:

♦ Compiling the guest list, including addresses and telephone numbers.

♦ Addressing invitations.

♦ Making decorations, name tags, place cards, and favors.

♦ Cooking or baking some of the food.

♦ Decorating.

♦ Arranging the gifts.

- Recording the gifts as they are opened (the name of the donor and what was given).

- Passing the gifts around the room for all the guests to see, being sure the cards stay with their corresponding gifts.

- Placing instant photos in an album to be given to the honored guests.

- Conducting the games, if any.

- Introducing the entertainment, if any.

- Serving the refreshments.

Chapter 16

Baby Shower "Detail Central"

These easy-to-use planning sheets are self-explanatory and are guaranteed to help you stay organized and within budget.

MASTER PLANNING SHEET

Name(s) of guest(s) of honor:

_____

Name(s) of co-host(s), if applicable:

_____

Date of party:

_____

Time of party:

_____

Location of party:

_____

Party's theme:

_____

Date invitations mailed:

_____

Type of food to be served:

_____

Games, activities, and entertainment:

_____   _____

_____   _____

_____   _____

_____   _____

GUEST LIST

Name	Address	Telephone #	Reply	
			yes	no

GUEST LIST, PAGE 2

Name	Address	Telephone #	Reply	
			yes	no

Total Attendees: _____

VOLUNTEERS

Name	Telephone #	Duty

PARTY SITE INFORMATION*

Name and location of site	
Name of contact person	
Telephone number	
Site rental fee	
Amount of deposit and date given	
Amount still due and due date	
Other fees (custodial, parking, coat attendant, etc.)	
Equipment available (tables, chairs, utensils, pots, pans, coffee pot, table linens, dishes, glasses, etc.)	
Equipment I will need to provide	
Restrictions (smoking, alcohol, loud music allowed, bringing in food and drink, etc.)	
Parking facilities—location and cost	

Total cost of site: $ _____

Transfer this amount to the master budget in Chapter 17.
*Photocopy one sheet for each site.

PARTY DECORATIONS

Item	Source	Cost
Flowers		
Balloons		
Streamers		
Baskets		
Candles		
Crepe paper		
Banners		
Acetate/fabric bows		
Tiny white strands		
Tulle netting		
Novelty decorations		
Other		

Total: $ _____

Transfer this amount to the master budget in Chapter 17.

TABLE DECORATIONS

Item	Source	Cost
Centerpiece		
Tablecloth		
Napkins		
Napkin rings		
Candles		
Cups/glassware		
Plates		
Utensils		
Place cards		
Favors		
Novelty decorations		
Other		

Total: $ _____

Transfer this amount to the master budget in Chapter 17.

GAME SUPPLIES

Game	Supplies	Cost
	_____	_____
	_____	_____
	_____	_____
	_____	_____
	_____	_____
	_____	_____
	_____	_____
	_____	_____
	_____	_____
	_____	_____
	_____	_____
	_____	_____
	_____	_____
	_____	_____
	_____	_____
Prizes: (including door prizes)	_____	_____
	_____	_____
	_____	_____
	_____	_____
	_____	_____

Total: $ _____

Transfer this amount to the master budget in Chapter 17.

PARTY MENU

Snacks and Appetizers

Item	To be prepared by	Cost

Soups

Item	To be prepared by	Cost

Salads

Item	To be prepared by	Cost

Sandwiches

Item	To be prepared by	Cost

Meat dishes

Item	To be prepared by	Cost

Side dishes

Item	To be prepared by	Cost

Breads

Item	To be prepared by	Cost

Condiments

Item	To be prepared by	Cost

Desserts

Item	To be prepared by	Cost

Drinks

Item	To be prepared by	Cost

Candies

Item	To be prepared by	Cost

Other

Item	To be prepared by	Cost

Total cost of party menu: $_____

Transfer this amount to the master budget in Chapter 17.

ENTERTAINMENT

Type	Provided by	Cost

Total: $ _____

Transfer this amount to the master budget in Chapter 17.

PARTY RENTALS

Item	Source with address and telephone	Cost

Total: $ _____

Transfer this amount to the master budget in Chapter 17.

WORDING FOR THE INVITATIONS

_____

_____

_____

_____

_____

_____

_____

_____

_____

_____

_____

_____

_____

Chapter 17

Baby Shower Money Minder

Spending more money doesn't necessarily mean your party will be more fun. You need to decide how much money you have available for hosting the party and then stay within that budget.

If you're high on "party spirit" but low on "party funds," here are a few suggestions:

- Hold the party in your home or any other *gratis* location.
- Ask others to co-host the party with you, which will ease the financial load.
- Choose an affordable theme.
- Serve punch or soft drinks instead of alcoholic beverages.
- Decorate with things you already have around the house, items that can be borrowed, or "big bangs for the buck" items, such as balloons and crepe paper streamers.
- Buy balloons in bulk from a party supply store and rent your own helium tank for blowing them up.
- Send informal invitations.

♦ Choose a theme that requires an affordable menu, such as a potluck picnic, or serve something easy, such as cake and coffee.

♦ Purchase food in bulk from a wholesale food supplier.

Master Budget

Note: Transfer the total costs from each category from the worksheets in Chapter 16 to this master budget.

Master Budget

Category	$ Amount budgeted	Final cost	Who pays?
Rental of party site			
Party decorations			
Table decorations			
Game supplies			
Party menu			
Entertainment			
Party rentals			
Other			

Total final cost: $ _____

Epilogue

I hope this book has filled your head with ideas for a lively, creative baby shower, inspired by a perfect theme that will tie everything together.

As you launch into your party plans, here are my three final words of advice:

1. Don't hesitate to ask friends to help you plan the party.
2. Once the party begins, keep it moving—don't give it a chance to bog down!
3. Relax and enjoy the party—and don't forget to smile!

Good luck,

Diane Warner

P.S. I will be updating this book from time to time and would love to hear about any interesting baby showers you may have planned or attended. Please write to me in care of my publisher:

> Diane Warner
> c/o Career Press
> P. O. Box 687
> Franklin Lakes, NJ 07417

Appendix

Patterns

Here is a variety of patterns you can use according to the theme you have chosen for your baby shower. Use them in creating the invitations, place cards, name tags, decorations, or favors. Enlarge the patterns on a photocopier as necessary to suit your purposes.

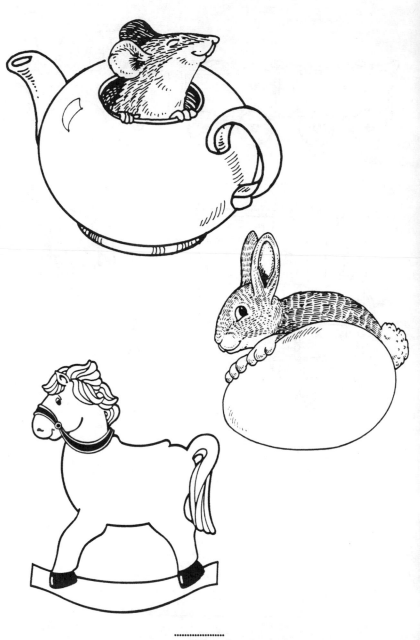

Index